P9-AGH-174

the Waves of Night and Other Stories

Other Books by Harry Mark Petrakis:

Novels

Lion at My Heart

The Odyssey of Kostas Volakis

A Dream of Kings

Short Stories

Pericles on 31st Street

Biography

The Founder's Touch

the Waves of Night and Other Stories

by Harry Mark Petrakis

David McKay Company, Inc., New York

the Waves of Night

and

Other Stories

Library of Congress Catalog Card Number: 74-81382

Manufactured in the United States of America

Dedication

for

Mark Van Doren

Acknowledgments

"*Rosemary*" © 1969 by Harry Mark Petrakis was first published in *Mademoiselle* in February, 1968.

"*The Sweet Life*" © 1969 by Harry Mark Petrakis was first published in *Confrontation,* Spring, 1968.

"*The Shearing of Samson*" © 1969 by Harry Mark Petrakis was first published in *U.S. Catholic,* November, 1967.

"*The Witness*" © 1969 by Harry Mark Petrakis was first published in *Playboy,* March, 1967.

"*End of Winter*" © 1969 by Harry Mark Petrakis was first published by *Cavalier,* October, 1962.

"*The Victim*" was first published in *U.S. Catholic,* May, 1966.

"*Dark Eye*" © 1969 by Harry Mark Petrakis was first published in *Playboy,* December, 1968.

Contents

Rosemary

Rosemary

"*I* must be nuts," Korshak, the white-haired railroad guard sitting at the counter, said. "Every meal I eat in here brings me a month closer to death."

"The complaint department is out the kitchen door and down the alley, third can from the right," Nick Manos, the lunchroom owner, said. He was a stocky, strong-bodied man in his late thirties, a soiled apron tied about his waist. He had dark unruly hair, a somber face, and even when cleanly shaven, his cheeks appeared shadowed.

"Ain't nothing wrong with this food," a tall, lean baggage handler named Noodles said, "long as your insurance premium is paid up."

Nick sighed. He scribbled on a pad and tore off a check that he put down in front of Korshak. "Eighty-six cents," he said.

The guard shook his head. "A shame I got to pay for a meal like that," he said sadly.

"You ate it," Nick said.

"I couldn't imagine it would taste as bad as it looked," Korshak winked.

4

"How much do I owe you, Nick?" Noodles slid off his stool.

"Sixty-three cents," Nick said. He shrugged wryly. "Sixty-three cents and eighty-six cents. If I ever get a customer with a check over a buck, I'll give him the place."

"He would want change," Korshak said sagely.

Noodles placed a few coins beside his check. "Guess I'll wash up later tonight after work," he said, and gave Nick a broad leer, "and drift around over to the Poinsetta Hotel."

"Better stay away from there, Noodles," Korshak warned. "That place full of tarts is due for a raid soon."

"Why don't you find a nice girl?" Nick said.

"Are there girls like that?" Noodles smirked.

"There are decent girls around," Nick said. "You meet one and get to know her and stop chasing whores."

Noodles laughed rejecting the advice and walked out to the dark street. Korshak brought his check to the register and put it down with a dollar bill. Nick rang up the amount and returned his change.

"About time to close up," Korshak said.

"Twenty more minutes," Nick said. "Just in time, too. By the end of the day this place becomes a prison."

He waved Korshak good night and walked along the counter to pick up the last dishes. He carried them to the kitchen and placed them on the shelf beside the battered metal sinks.

He stood for a moment over the sinks seeing the whole shabby and squalid lunchroom reflected in the rancid water. The place had been owned by his father for twenty years until his death six years earlier when Nick inherited it. He had made a few halfhearted efforts to scrub the floor and paint the walls. Then he gave up and consoled himself he could really do nothing with the aged stains of gravies and soups on the floor boards, the strong smells of wilted vegetables, the crusts of dried hard grease on the stove, the scarred and unmendable counter and stools. He planned to hold the place just long enough to build a small stake and then dump it for whatever he could get. But without his father's capacity to salvage and utilize scraps, he barely made enough on which to live and a little more to give his mother who lived with his married sister. In addition, as time went on he found himself forced to work longer hours every day in an effort to achieve even that meager return.

He bent savagely and dipped his hands into the dish-water and saw his blurred image among the particles of food and whorls of grease floating on the surface. He considered draining the sink and running in fresh water but decided against the additional delay.

When he finished the last dishes, he drained the water and dried his hands. He carried a broom out to the front to sweep the floor. He was surprised to see a young woman sitting at the far end of the counter.

"I'm sorry, lady," Nick said. "I didn't hear you come in."

"I heard you working in the kitchen and didn't want to bother you," the girl said. "All I want is a cup of coffee."

He filled a cup of coffee from the urn and carried it to her. The only women who patronized his place in the shadow of the trucking depots and the railroad terminal were the assemblers and coilers from the factory across the street. They were beefy-armed, robust-breasted women with huge rumps that engulfed the stools. This girl was slim and no more than twenty-three or twenty-four. Her face was pale, her features even and small, her eyes large and dark. Her hair was dark brown and long and she wore a narrow band of black velvet across her crown, a band studded with tiny stars.

The band was strangely familiar and then as if the past were a crust that suddenly shattered he remembered a girl he had known when he was a young boy. He could not remember her name but they had skated together in the winter on the frozen ponds, whirling and laughing, their arms holding one another, their breath joining swift spirals of mist in the cold clear air. She had worn a short red skating skirt, white stockings, a fur-collared jacket, and in her hair a black velvet band studded with tiny stars.

Still unsettled by nostalgia, he finished sweeping the floor and then wiped the pie case. He closed at ten and when he looked at the clock again it was a few minutes past that time. The girl was smoking over her coffee, lost in reveries of her own. He walked to the door and flicked the switch that turned off the light above the sign outside and darkened the row of small lights in the window. When he turned back she had risen from the stool.

"Time to go," she said. With a nervous flutter of her fingers she crushed the tip of her cigarette into an ashtray. She wore a dark cloth coat and she tugged the collar higher about her throat and stared with foreboding out at the street. He felt sorry for her.

7

"I won't be leaving for a few minutes yet," Nick said. "Have another cup of coffee on the house before I empty the urn."

She looked at him gratefully and then nodded slowly and sat down. He brought her another cup of coffee and watched her begin to sip it. The coffee moistened her lips and they were full and well curved with a tiny cleft in one corner. She caught him staring and he turned brusquely to finish his work. He emptied the urn and put in a fresh bag for morning. She finished her coffee and brought him the cup and saucer. Then she fumbled in her purse for change. He waved her money aside.

"It's on the house."

"Thank you."

"You live close by?" he asked and was startled by the loudness of his voice. "I mean it's late and do you have a car?"

He sensed a sudden distress about her. She was silent for a long moment before she answered.

"I don't live in the city," she said. She stared through the plate-glass window at the railroad station looming above the roofs of the buildings across the street. "I was supposed to meet someone earlier today. A soldier who was coming from out of town, too. I was to have met him at two this afternoon." The illuminated clock in the tower of the station had black hands shining at twenty minutes past ten.

"He could have had his leave canceled," Nick said. "That happens, you know."

"I knew by late afternoon he wasn't coming," she said slowly. "I waited even though I knew he wasn't coming."

8

A truck rumbled past on the narrow darkened street and the old wooden floor quivered slightly under their feet. A gust of wind whipped a shred of newspaper against the window. It hung there a moment and then whirled off.

"You know anybody in the city you can phone?" Nick asked. "I mean do you have any family or friends here?"

She shook her head. A slight tremor swept her shoulders. He wondered uneasily if she were going to cry.

"I'll walk over to the station," she said, "and wait for a train back home. I think there is one in a couple of hours."

"Just wait a minute now," he frowned and stood thinking for a moment. "I'm just closing. I'll walk you back to the station. This isn't the neighborhood for a girl to walk around at night."

He walked quickly to the kitchen, pulling off his apron on the way. He made sure the back door was locked and got his coat from the locker. He snapped off the remaining lights, completely darkening the lunchroom except for a small bulb that threw an eerie beam over the desolate counters and stools.

She moved aside and he opened the door. A gust of cold air chilled their ankles. He locked the door and they started walking toward the railroad station.

"I'm glad to get out of that place," he said. "My father owned it, worked it eighteen hours for twenty years until he died."

"Do you work it that way, too?"

Another truck rumbled by sweeping their bodies with twin beams of light. From the railroad yards a bell tolled a sharp harsh sound. He shivered and pushed his hands deeper into the pockets of his coat.

"I made the old man a promise to stick it out and I've got my mother to support. But I have other plans. A good friend of mine has been writing me to come help him run a big fancy hotel in Denver with several hundred rooms. He wants me to manage the restaurant and bar. I'm planning to go soon."

At the corner he took her elbow and through her coat felt the firm young flesh of her arm. He was seized by a flutter of unrest in his stomach. They walked up the stairs to the station and he noticed her legs were long and slender in sheer nylons and high-heeled pumps.

They entered the large station waiting room, gray walls and concrete floors and worn benches, the air stale with old smoke and rancid steam from the radiators. The waiting room was almost deserted except for a few soldiers and sailors sleeping on some of the benches, duffel and sea bags cradling their heads. A porter swept a mop across a segment of the concrete floor with a weary flinging motion of his arms. Beyond the waiting room were the ticket windows, all closed but one, a bald man suspended within the lighted square.

"There might be a message for you with the agent," he said.

She nodded slowly and he watched her walking toward the ticket window on her slender legs, her back slim and straight. He wondered whether the soldier and the girl were lovers and jealousy bit his flesh. He moved toward a bench away from those occupied by the sleeping servicemen and after a few moments she joined him.

"There's no message," she said. "I didn't think there would be."

She spoke softly and calmly, sorrow apparent only in her voice, and he admired her restraint.

"When does your train leave?" he asked.

She opened her purse and drew out a small red ticket stamped for Champaign, Illinois. "In an hour and a half," she said.

"I'll wait with you, if it's O.K."

"You don't have to stay," she said. "You must be tired. I'll be all right now."

He shrugged. "I'm used to it."

She sat down at the end of the bench and he sat down beside her, making sure a few inches of the bench was visible between their bodies. They sat without speaking for a few moments. He stole several glances at her face, noting the strange weary and uneasy lines around her mouth. He felt a flare of indignation at the man who let her wait in the station alone.

"Do you like stations?" she asked.

"I don't know," he said. "I don't have any feeling about them one way or another."

"I love to come and just sit in them," she said. "I do it sometimes even when I don't have anyplace to go. I make believe I'm going on a trip, or that I have just returned, and that family and friends are going to meet me. You ever noticed how happy people who travel are?" He shook his head.

"It's usually true," she said. "They're going to visit friends or relatives or going on vacations. For a while there may be separations but then the reunions are joyful."

"I never thought of it that way," he said. "I guess you're right."

"It isn't always true," she said quietly. "Sometimes there is unhappiness, too. And then there are the soldiers and sailors like those asleep over there. They have to go where they are sent, from one camp to another, and then perhaps overseas, away from their families and sweethearts for a long time." She shook her head. "Some of them are just kids."

"You're not much more than a kid yourself," he smiled.

She answered with a brusque short laugh.

"I mean it," he said. "How old are you?"

"Twenty-three," she said. "And you?"

"Thirty-six," he said and felt foolish because he had cut a year and then regretted he had not severed several more. "I'm thirty-six and still unmarried," he shrugged wryly.

She studied him for a long moment and he grew uneasy under her gaze.

"Someday a fortunate girl is going to get you," she said.

He looked at her sharply, wondering if she were mocking him.

"It's true," she said gravely. "When you offered me the second cup of coffee so I could stay inside a little longer and when you walked me here to the station because you were concerned something might happen to me, I knew you were something special."

"That was nothing," he said.

12

"You were kind," she said slowly. "Kindness is rare and when you have it you are someone special."

"That's enough about me," he said, and his voice came out strong and jubilant. "You know I don't even know your name?"

She smiled and he felt the two of them drawn closer.

"Rosemary," she said.

"That's a lovely name."

"Some people hate their names," she said, "and wish they had been called by another. But I have always thought Rosemary sounds like a flower."

He nodded and spoke softly under his breath. "Mine is Nick," he said. "Not much of a name but I'm stuck with it. Actually it's Nicholas."

"I like Nicholas better than Nick," she said. "But I suppose everybody calls you Nick?"

"Nick and a lot of other things," he laughed. "Most of my trade are railroad workers and baggage handlers and truck drivers. Rough, maybe, but good guys."

"They must like you," she said. "They must come to talk to you if they have troubles."

He remembered her grief and it sobered his pleasure. He looked at the young sleeping soldiers.

"Sometimes it helps to talk," he said. "But you don't have to talk about your friend if you don't want to."

"I don't mind talking about him," she said quietly. She put her hands together in her lap and he saw how meagerly the flesh hinged across the wrists.

"I'm not bitter or angry with him, either," she said. "In the beginning after we first met, he wrote me almost every day. Beautiful letters that I will always treasure. In the last two months he wrote me only twice. I felt he had met another girl, loved her as he had once loved me, and I wrote asking for the truth. At first he denied it and then we agreed to meet in the station today, to talk over what we were going to do." She spoke softly, her voice barely more than a whisper, and he leaned slightly closer to hear. "He must have felt this way would be easier than having to tell me," she said. "I don't blame him, and I'm not bitter. Shall I tell you why?"

He nodded although he found it hard to understand why she should not have been angry.

"Even if I had known it would end like this," she said, "waiting for hours in a station and taking a train home alone, even if I had known, I wouldn't have given up a single hour of the time we had together, the letters, or the dreams." He saw her face with its spare flesh stretched tightly over small bones, a redness in the corners of her eyes. "True love is worth any sorrow and any grief and I will remember as long as I live that I had such love for a little while."

He heard the anguish in her voice and the loneliness and he was moved. He closed his eyes for a moment, locking himself in darkness.

"I understand," he said. "I had love like that once, too. A girl I was going to marry years ago. She became ill and died." He opened his eyes and looked at her. A quick and tender compassion for him swept her face.

"It happened years ago," he said. "I think I loved her in the way you speak of because I have never been able to feel the same about anyone else since. I think of her now at different times during the day but mostly at night, after a long tired day in the lunchroom, at night when I can't sleep and wonder what my life would be like if she had lived."

They were both silent for a moment and then she moved her hand from her lap, slowly, bringing it to rest on his wrist, her slim fingers touching his arm lightly in consolation. The moment passed and she drew her hand away. He was embarrassed and grateful when the hoarse almost unintelligible voice of a man sounded over the loud-speaker announcing the arrival of a train. A soldier on one of the benches raised his head like a startled bird and then lowered it slowly to the bag on the bench. A redcap emerged from a baggage room and walked leisurely toward the gate.

"Maybe you're hungry," he said cheerfully. "The refreshment counter is closed but they've got vending machines in an alcove. I can get you a sandwich and a Coke if you like, or maybe some candy."

"I'm not hungry, but thanks," she said and smiled. He smiled at her and felt his weariness lifted like a rock from his back.

"You know it's strange," he said. "Strange the way we've met. Do you know what I mean? It's almost like fate, you coming into the lunchroom just a few minutes before I closed and coming back here together and talking like this."

"I believe in fate," she said, and smiled again. "Maybe there's something here neither of us can understand." She looked down at her fingers in her lap. "Both of us sharing a grief and a memory of love," she said gravely.

They fell silent and he looked with concern at the clock. There was so little time before her train. Yet Champaign was only a few hours away and he imagined himself driving down for a weekend. He felt a quick sharp excitement through his body.

"Rosemary," he said. "This may sound crazy because we just met tonight, and I know how you feel about this young man, and I'm a good deal older than you . . . but I wonder if I could write to you . . . just a letter or two in the beginning . . ."

He was interrupted by a noisy outburst of voices in shouts and laughter. A group of half a dozen men had entered through one of the gates, loudly roistering their way through the station.

"Some of the guys from the yards," he said resenting the distraction, "on their way for a beer." He turned back to her feeling a flurry of panic because he might have assumed too much, pressed too quickly against a still raw grief.

"You don't have to write me back if you don't feel like it," he said. "But I'd like to write you a few letters so you can get to know me better. When I go to Denver I can write you what my experiences are and whenever you feel like dropping me a short note you can let me know how you are, too."

The men drew closer and he recognized a casual patron or two and one nodded and the other waved his hand in a brief greeting. Then the lean wry face of Noodles emerged from the group, as he fell a step behind the others when he spotted Nick.

"Hi ya, Nick, boy," he cried loudly. "Skipping town to evade the Health Department?" He noticed the girl and fell silent. A surprised and twisted smirk crossed his cheeks. "Hello, Netta," he said. He winked and pursed his lips. "Take good care of Nick, will you?" He grinned and rolled his eyes. "He's a buddy of mine." He moved off after the men who had reached the door. They all left the station.

For a moment Nick did not move. There was a stunned fumbling in his head and a whirling of sound in his ears. Sweat erupted across his back and chest. He rose from the bench and he felt himself trembling. "Jesus Christ," he said, and the words came slurred from his lips. "Jesus Christ."

She looked up at him with her face shocked as his, her cheeks white as gravestones, her lips frozen.

"Are you crazy?" Nick said hoarsely. "Is this some kind of goddamn joke?"

She shook her head numbly and a great shudder swept her body.

"I didn't mean any harm," she said, and the words stumbled in a frantic whisper from her lips. "I just came in for a cup of coffee and you were nice to me and I just started making things up. . . . I swear to God I didn't mean any harm."

He felt an outrage at her deceit, and even more anger at his own gullibility. She had tricked him, cheated him into exposing himself, duped him into pleading. He reached down and snatched the purse from her side. He snapped open the clasp and reached in and drew out the ticket.

"What the hell did you buy the ticket for?" he cried in a low harsh voice. "Ride there and ride all the way back so you could carry the trick right through to the end! Have me see you off, have me put you on the god-damn train and wave goodbye so that you could laugh all the way to Champaign and back! You must be nuts!"

In a wild eruption of fury he tore the ticket into shreds and threw the pieces on the floor at her feet.

She stared down at the floor as if he had torn her up as well. She bent slowly and picked up one of the fragments. He saw the band of stars in her hair and felt a furious urge to tear it from her head. She looked back up at him with her face like a mask of death.

"You goddamn lying whore!" he said. He twisted away from her and hurried from the station.

He wandered the dark cold streets around the depot for a long time. A wind carrying the chill of the frozen lake whipped his flushed cheeks. Anger died slowly in little spasms within him. He passed the lunchroom and looked with a sudden loathing at the shadowed interior, the dingy counters, the battered coffee urn. In less than five hours he would be back in that prison again.

He walked to the boulevard that ran parallel to the park. He passed under the gaunt trees, his shadow sweeping the deserted benches that glittered under the swaying street lights. The wind blew scraps of newspaper around the base of the stone monument erected to some heroic dead. He shivered and the station clock struck twelve, the resonant peals lingering in the desolate night.

He climbed the stairs to the bridge over the maze of tracks, rested his elbows on the ledge in the center, and listened to the banging of freight cars being shunted in the dark yards below. He looked up, trying to make out the clarity of a star against the darkness of the sky but suddenly the frail paleness of Rosemary's face intruded before his eyes.

He closed his eyes tightly for a moment and when he opened them he stared at the buildings gleaming in the distance, lighted tiny windows still resembling remote stars. Something closer caught his attention and over the bare frozen branches and boughs of trees a mile or so away he saw a clearing with a glistening pond of ice. He could just make out the small dark forms of a boy and girl skating together, the two of them alone on the pond. They moved as if locked by their arms, skimming in circles around the pond until the girl broke free and whirled gracefully alone.

He leaned forward on the bridge imagining he could hear the shrill whistling of her skates on the ice, almost see her face sparkling with the joy of her flight. He felt his heart straining to join her, to share her delight. He was seized suddenly with trembling.

He left the bridge, retraced his walk leaving the park, and hurried back to the station. He walked up the stairs and entered the doors, with his blood pulsing. When he saw she was gone, the bench where they had been, empty, he almost cried out.

Confused and uncertain what to do next, he thought of

finding Noodles. Then he recalled the Poinsetta Hotel where she might have a room.

He walked quickly down to the street again, passed the lunchroom without a glance, crossed the boulevard entering the settlement of small dingy hotels, dim smoky taverns, and strip joints masquerading as clubs. When he saw the misted amber sign of the Poinsetta Hotel, he ran until he reached it. He entered the lobby short of breath. A night clerk with cheeks like granite and eyes like chips of stone sat behind the desk reading a newspaper.

"Is Netta here?" Nick asked.

The clerk raised his head for a moment. A slight stiff curl of his lips denied the name. He looked back at his paper.

"I'm not a cop," Nick said. "I work right here in the neighborhood. I know her."

The clerk kept his eyes on the paper.

"Listen," Nick said desperately. "Noodles is a friend of mine. He told me to ask for her."

The clerk studied him for a long hard instant. He motioned finally toward a house phone around the side of the desk. He left his chair and as Nick picked up the receiver, he plugged in a line at the switchboard. There was a buzzing in the receiver and Nick held his breath. When he heard her voice, a small fire cut the darkness.

"This is Nick," he said. "Nick Manos."

She did not answer.

"I want to see you, please," he said. "I want to come up for a minute."

20

There was another tight moment of silence and then he heard her voice, quiet and without emotion.

"Room 314," she said.

He hung up the phone and walked toward the elevator. The door was open and he entered, pushed the button for three, and the doors closed. The elevator creaked and whined up.

On the third floor he emerged into a faintly lit corridor. A phonograph wailed a scratched tuneless melody carrying from a nearby room. He peered closely at one of the numbers and then saw a feeble square of light at the end of the corridor. He walked slowly toward it.

The door was open and Netta stood inside a narrow room lit only by the gloomy light from a tiny lamp on a bedstand behind her. He could make out the bed, a dresser, and an armchair. Her face was shrouded in shadow and she wore a quilted robe that hung to her ankles. Her feet were bare, slim and white on the darker carpet, the toes like small shining shells.

He hesitated a moment and then stepped into the room. He closed the door behind him. Almost at once he breathed the scent of some strange perfume, an odor of withered flowers or musty leaves.

"There is something I want to tell you," he said, and his words whispered like an echo. "I've been walking around for a long time and I had to come and tell you I'm sorry. I'm sorry for what I said."

She stood concealed in shadow and silence and he tried to see within the shrouded hollows and circles of her face.

"There is something else, too," he said. "I'm not stuck

in the lunchroom because it was my father's dying wish. I'm stuck in it because I'm lazy and worthless and don't know what else I want to do. I don't have any ambition and I don't have any hope."

The silence tightened and drew thin between them. She did not move or make a sound. The spread on the bed reflected tiny metallic points of light.

"I don't have any friend in Denver who owns a fancy hotel," he said, "and who wants me to handle the restaurant and bar. The only job I been offered in the past five years was to take bets for a bookie who hangs out in the men's room of the railroad station."

He had a sense of the wretched months and years moving past his lips, falling with an ache from his flesh. He looked down at the scuffed worn tips of his shoes.

"The girl I might have married years ago," he said. "She didn't get sick and die. She became pregnant and I would have married her but I was afraid that the kid wasn't mine. She had an abortion and couldn't stand the sight of me afterward. I don't know where she is now."

His voice fell away and he finished in a futile silence.

For an instant it seemed something stirred under the shadowed flesh of her cheeks. Then she moved around and walked a few steps to the other side of the bed. She turned back to him.

He saw her face in the gleam of the lamp and she appeared a stranger. The flesh puffed slightly about the eyes, the skin of her cheeks gray and sallow, the hair dull and lank. But it was her eyes that were altered the most, hard cold buds suspended between the womb and the grave.

22

"I'm a whore not a priest," she said, and the words came frozen and quiet from her lips. "If you want to stick around, it's ten bucks a jump."

He looked at her and tried to answer. The words stuck in his throat. He heard a moan beginning somewhere deep in his body and as it sought to burst from his heart, he turned for the door and fled.

the Sweet Life

the Sweet Life

Mark and Jerry had gone to see the film "La Dolce Vita" a few days before they were to return to Michigan State for the fall semester. They first noticed the two girls in the lobby of the theatre during the intermission. Both girls were dark-haired, one tall and large-breasted with long strong legs and the other girl slender and smaller. She had a fragile high-cheeked face and great dark eyes and her black hair was brushed back into a simple coiled bun that gave her a smoldering Castilian beauty.

They were both smoking up a fog and talking loudly about the picture in a way that demanded to be noticed. Jerry worked his way over to them and Mark followed him. Jerry asked them with his swinging charm if they weren't a couple of Italian starlets touring with the picture for publicity purposes. They started laughing and the big girl, Norma, had a hoarse and throaty laugh and Senta laughed with a soft quivering of her lips around her small even white teeth. By the time the intermission was over they had made arrangements to meet after the movie. On the way back to their seats Mark and Jerry counted their money and agreed that Jerry had Norma while Mark would take Senta.

When the lights went on at the end of the film, the boys hurried through the press of people up the aisle. The girls were waiting for them in the lobby and they walked over to Rush Street and entered a tavern and sat down in a shadowed booth. Norma ordered a Bloody Mary and Senta ordered a Daiquiri. The waiter asked to see her I.D. card. Jerry and Norma teased her as she dug irritably into her purse and showed the card to the waiter. Mark learned she was nineteen and a junior at Ohio State. Mark and Jerry ordered beer.

"I liked the ending of the picture," Senta said. "The marvelous expression on the little girl's face as she called to Marcello."

"She resented missing the party," Jerry said. "She wanted Marcello so they could have a party of their own."

Norma laughed loudly in appreciation and Jerry joined her, pleased with his wit. Senta made an effort to laugh politely but it didn't quite come off and Mark felt drawn to her because of her reaction.

"That perfectly horrible fish," Norma shuddered in disgust. "That round dead eye staring up at them. It made my skin crawl. What kind of fish was that?"

"A schooner fish," Jerry said.

"The fish was a symbol," Mark said. "A bloated monster reflecting the uselessness of their own lives."

Jerry grinned and motioned at Mark. "When he graduates next June he wants to become a writer like Marcello," he said. "I think his real reason is that he wants to go to parties like that blast in the film."

"I think he looks a little like Marcello," Senta said.

"The hell he does," Jerry snickered.

"More like the fish," Mark said.

"I mean it," Senta said seriously. "You have the same sensitive eyes."

"Don't let that sensitive look fool you," Jerry said. "He uses that look to draw a girl into his web and then . . ."

"Cut it out," Mark said.

The waiter brought their drinks. They cheerfully toasted each other. Jerry took a long swill of beer and shifted closer to Norma who made no effort to slide away.

"The best scene in the picture was that party," Jerry said. "That crazy doll who did the strip and those fairies prancing around and Marcello trying to paste the chicken feathers all over the blonde."

"Remember the way she flapped her arms," Norma said. She flapped her own firm bare arms and crowed, "Oo-oo-ahroo!"

"Take it easy," Mark said. "They'll throw us out of here."

"It was sure a great party," Jerry said. "Maybe I can get the guys in the frat house to throw one like it."

"Be sure to invite me," Norma said.

"I'll invite you right now," Jerry slipped his arm around her shoulders, "and let you know the date later on." They both exploded into laughter and Mark looked wryly at Senta.

"I've been to some pretty good parties myself," Norma said with a smirk.

"The hell you say," Jerry said. "Tell us about them."

"You college rah-rahs ever hear of musical chairs?" Norma laughed. "Well, I have played the same game with beds."

Jerry chortled with delight. He let his hand slip over Norma's shoulder, his fingers hanging very near her breast.

"She's just showing off," Senta said sharply to Jerry. "She has a good job in an advertising office and helps support her mom and dad."

"Mama doesn't think a girl needs any fun after a day's work in a lousy office," Norma gave Senta a quick bitter look. "After we graduated from high school, Senta was able to go on to college but I had to go to work. That doesn't mean I have to sit home and feel my arteries hardening."

"Not if I can help it, doll," Jerry said soothingly. He signaled the waiter to bring another round of drinks.

"Let's talk about the movie," Senta said with a silent plea to Mark. The dim lights of the tavern threw restless shadows across her pale cheeks and dark eyes. "I thought Fellini did a marvelous job, a kind of parable of the emptiness of our materialistic culture."

"It was all right," Norma said, "but I still think it was a pretty dirty picture."

"It wasn't dirty at all," Mark said. "It was a very moral portrayal of immorality."

"Don't tell me he had to go into that much loving detail to make a moral point," Norma snickered. "All those nymphomaniacs and homosexuals and fairies."

"Fairies and homosexuals are the same thing," Jerry said.

"I know that," Norma gave him a slight playful shove. "Don't you think I know that?"

"Mark is right," Senta said. "There were many haunting and beautiful scenes that I will never forget."

"I liked the scenes with Steiner," Mark said.

"Why did Steiner kill himself?" Norma asked.

"I'm not sure why," Senta said.

"I'm not sure either," Mark said. "He seems to have had everything a man could want. A beautiful family, literary success and artistic friends. But he was terrified of something no one else could see."

"I liked the part where Marcello's old man visits him," Jerry said. "He lectures Marcello about sin and then wants to go to a nightclub where the old rip begins to fondle one of the dolls in the chorus. He sure reminded me of my old man. I know for a fact he's had at least a half-dozen girlfriends in the last ten years. I wouldn't be surprised if my old lady knew it too even though all she cares about is playing cards five nights a week."

"There's been a change in the structure of society," Senta said. "Marital loyalty for fifty years to the same person is sheer hypocrisy."

"Now who is showing off?" Norma asked loudly.

"I mean it!" Senta said and her eyes flashed. "In Hollywood movies, sex is a daydream for people who are scared they will never find the real thing. In French and Italian movies the people don't moon around wondering what sex is really like. If they want sex, they have it, and when they are done they forget about it until next time. It's more honest that way."

"I think you gals are both a little too fast for us," Jerry said and winked at Mark. He tried to catch the waiter's attention.

"I don't think we'd better have any more to drink," Mark said. He figured their combined funds would about cover the drinks they already had.

"If you're short I know how it is," Senta said. "Norma and I will be glad to share the bill."

"Speak for yourself, honey," Norma said. "That might be the way you little college girls do it, but I work hard for my money."

"We wouldn't consider it anyway," Jerry said and grinned. "I've got a better idea. My folks are in Washington. My old lady goes along on the old man's business trips to keep an eye on him. Our house is empty and the bar is loaded."

Senta gave Norma a long warning look. "I'm staying with Norma at her house," she said. "Her mom and dad asked us not to be late."

"By this time mama and papa will be sound asleep," Norma said, "their fannies snuggled and both snoring like bears." She smiled coyly at Jerry. "My papa is faithful to my mama," she said, "but he does have a cabinet full of nude girlie photos in the basement."

"What does your mama do for kicks?" Jerry asked with a snicker.

"She adores Cary Grant," Norma said. "She sees all his pictures at least a half-dozen times and dreams about him almost every night."

"They'll never miss you then," Jerry said. "C'mon let's go."

Norma looked hesitantly for a moment at Senta and then shrugged and rose. "I don't feel sleepy yet anyway," she said. "Tomorrow's Saturday and we don't have to get up till late."

They paid the check and left the tavern. Jerry walked with his arm around Norma's waist, his fingers spread slightly on her thigh. Senta and Mark walked slowly behind them.

"They sure hit it off well together," Mark said. They walked in silence for a few moments. The summer night was marked with a trace of early burning leaves.

"Norma is a fine girl," Senta said. "She was my best friend in high school. We used to talk all night. She was terribly disappointed when she couldn't go to college."

"You are both very different," Mark said.

Senta was silent and when she finally spoke, her voice was pensive. "Two years can be a long time," she said. "I can even see the change at home. My mother and father think I have grown callous and hard. My father is a pharmacist and thinks all life can be reduced to the exact measure for a prescription."

"I know what you mean," Mark said. "After my second year in college I couldn't stand the whole summer at home. I took jobs in other cities. It seemed I couldn't say or do anything anymore without hurting my parents in some way."

They turned off Rush Street and left the bright noisy cafes. A wind came off the lake and blew the scent of burning leaves more strongly about their heads. Mark studied Senta's face in the light of a passing streetlamp.

"You're lovely," he said suddenly. "You're a very lovely girl." He couldn't tell whether she was pleased. "I bet you've heard that from many fellows before me."

"I don't object when someone tells me that I'm pretty," Senta said quietly, "but looks can be a handicap too. Men can be distracted by surface allure and forget a girl is also a human being."

"I understand that," Mark said quickly. "In addition to beauty you have a sharp and sensitive mind."

He could tell that pleased her and after a moment he took her hand. They walked a short way in silence.

"I enjoy reading a great deal," Senta said.

"What writers do you like?"

"Tolstoy and Dostoevski in the novel and Sartre in the drama," Senta said. "A lot of poetry but mostly the work of Pablo Neruda."

"I don't know him," Mark said. "I guess I should, but I don't."

"He's a great Chilean poet," Senta said. "And I love foreign films and my favorite actress is Sophia Loren . . . she's a woman in every sense of the word."

They reached the lot where Jerry had parked the car and could not see him or Norma. They walked to the car and saw the figures in the shadowed front seat curled in a tight embrace. Mark looked at Senta with a faint embarrassed smile and knocked on the windshield. Jerry and Norma disengaged themselves slowly and Jerry motioned for them to get in the back. Mark held the door open for Senta and climbed in after her.

"I'm sorry we disturbed you," Mark said with sarcasm.

"Never mind," Jerry laughed. "We can always pick up where we left off."

They pulled into the driveway of Jerry's house, a large spacious ranch building on a lot landscaped with evergreens and myriad trees. Norma gave a low whistle of appreciation.

"It's all right," Jerry shrugged. "The old man takes the suckers for plenty in his law practice."

He drove straight for the garage and the door opened. He parked the sport coupe beside a long gleaming Cadillac. On the dark steps before entering the kitchen Jerry walked behind Norma and suddenly she squealed. "You naughty boy!" she cried.

They passed through a long kitchen with a massive twin-doored refrigerator and a stainless steel stove into a living-room paneled in walnut with an imposing array of lamps and sculpture.

"Lovely," Norma said with awe. "Just lovely."

"Wait till you see this," Jerry said. He walked to a corner and pushed a button. The wall panel slid back to reveal a compact bar with a glittering assortment of glasses and bottles.

"Better than any Rush Street tavern," Norma marveled. "If it's for real, make me another Bloody Mary."

Jerry moved briskly behind the bar and began mixing the drink. Senta sat down stiffly on the couch.

"What will you have?" Mark asked her.

"I don't think I want another drink," she said.

"Come on, honey," Jerry said. "Give me a chance to show how good a bartender I am."

"I just don't want another drink," Senta said.

"I'll take scotch on the rocks," Mark said.

When Jerry had finished mixing their drinks he picked up a glass and a nearly full bottle of bourbon and came out from behind the bar. He stood looking at Norma with his broad shoulders hunched slightly and a reckless glint in his eyes. "I'm taking my bottle upstairs," he said slowly. "Anybody want to see the bedrooms?"

Mark looked uneasily at Senta. "For cri' sakes slow down," he said to Jerry.

Jerry loosed a short brusque snicker. "What the hell for? We sat in the bar an hour and a half. We all know why we came here. Let's not waste the whole damn night sparring around." He motioned with the bottle to Norma. "Coming, doll?"

Norma glanced hesitantly at Senta.

"Or was all that talk about musical beds just showing off," Jerry said. "The little working girl trying to impress the college crowd."

Norma turned back to Jerry with a defiant glitter in her eyes.

"You could at least put on some damn music," Mark said to Jerry.

"You play all the mood music you want," Jerry said in

a flat hard voice. "Read some poetry too. Spend the whole damn night talking. I'm going upstairs now."

Senta gave him a scathing contemptuous look but he ignored her. Norma rose slowly from her chair and stood a moment staring at Senta. "Enjoy yourself, honey," Norma said in a tight and brittle voice. "La Dolce Vita."

She turned then and started up the stairs, carrying her drink, her firm thighs pressing against the skirt of her dress. Conscious of them watching her she affected a certain casual disdain. Jerry started after her with a cool smile of triumph. "The first floor is all yours," he said to Mark. He followed Norma upstairs.

Mark watched him out of sight and glanced uneasily at Senta. She sat a little stiffly in silence and after a moment laughed shortly.

"He must be the prize bull of sorority row," she said.

"He does pretty well."

"And how about you?" Senta said. "Do you do pretty well too?"

"Not nearly as well as Jerry," Mark said. He took a long swallow of scotch.

"You're the sensitive kind," Senta said.

"Sure," Mark said sharply. "That's why I brought you here."

"You didn't bring me," Senta said. "Your fast friend brought me. You just came along."

"All right," Mark said. "Don't bite my head off. I'm not going to attack you. You can just relax and read a good book until your friend comes down."

Senta rose and walked to the fireplace. She stood for an

instant with her back to him and then whirled around. Her dark eyes glistened angrily.

"I'll do what I want to do!" she said. "The whole business isn't that important. If only people would stop hacking at it like woodchoppers and show a little grace."

"Okay, okay," Mark said. "Your friend is over twenty-one but I'm sorry we came here. I didn't mean to hurt your feelings."

The tight angry circles loosened slightly in her face. She returned to the couch and sat down.

"Do you believe in fate?" Senta asked quietly.

"In what way?"

"Do you believe that whatever happens to us is predestined to happen long before we are born?"

"I don't think I buy that," Mark said.

"I feel that way about love," Senta said. "That I will find it someday as it was planned long before my life began." She looked so lovely, the shadows sweeping her face and her lips gleaming. Mark leaned over suddenly and kissed her, feeling her lips surprisingly soft under his mouth.

He pulled back sharply expecting her to protest. She sat looking at him quietly without a trace of warmth in the firm carved lines around her mouth.

He kissed her again pressing his lips harder over her mouth. She twisted in his arms and he thought he felt her kissing him back. A wild urgency caught at his body and he pulled her against him in a hard embrace that robbed them both of breath. He felt the agitation of her heart. His hand rose to touch the trembling swell of her small firm breast and she began to struggle. For an instant he thought it was because she was excited until he realized she was fighting him. He paused in surprise still holding her arms.

"What's the matter?" he asked.

She looked at him with her dark eyes open so wide they resembled cups. "I won't!" she said.

"What?"

"I won't!" she cried. "I won't!"

He had heard those words as a prelude before and he ignored them and bent to kiss her again. She began to struggle violently and he was startled at the strength in her slim body. He fought to hold her and suddenly she went limp in his arms. After a moment he relaxed his grip. Almost at once she cried out and with a hard vengeful sweep of her arm raked his cheek with her nails, tearing his flesh. He cried out in shock and pain and slipped to his knees beside the couch holding his torn cheek.

"Oh my God, I'm sorry," she said. "I'm so sorry." She sat there pale and scared, her blouse pulled askew showing the flesh of her shoulder.

Mark rose slowly to his feet. "That's all right," he said and his voice sounded strange in his ears. He turned and started from the room.

"Where are you going?" she asked quickly.

"To get some iodine," he said. "Do you mind?" He walked to the bathroom. He snapped on the lights and the faces that stared back at him from the multiple mirrors did not seem his own. The scratch ran an ugly red scar down his cheek. He washed it, grimacing with pain, and then found a bottle of iodine in the cabinet.

38

"Let me do that, please." She had come to stand quietly in the doorway. She didn't wait for him to answer but took the bottle from his hand. She began to apply the dauber to the long scratch.

"Take it easy," he said wincing.

"I'm sorry," she said.

"That's about the tenth time you've said you're sorry," he said with sarcasm. "Change the broken record."

When she finished applying the iodine, he looked at himself in the mirror.

"I look like a goddamn Indian," he said dejectedly. "I don't know how I'm going to explain this to Jerry."

"Can't you tell him you cut yourself shaving?"

"Cut myself like this?" he asked. "Are you nuts? What do you think I shave with, a saber?"

They stared at each other and her lips quivered in a faint smile.

"Go ahead and laugh," he said angrily. "If you had scratched Jerry like this, he would probably have beaten hell out of you."

"You're not Jerry," she said. "That's why I like you."

"God, I'm lucky," he said and loosed a short harsh laugh. "You like me so Jerry gets laid and I get a torn face to carry around like a badge of honor for days."

She stood watching him and he noticed the sadness of her eyes. She raised her hand and touched his cheek, her fingers fluttering softly as a bird's wing beneath the raw red line of the scratch. He had a strange feeling that she was touching the bone beneath the flesh of his face.

Something in her fingertips made him reach uncertainly

for her again. She raised her small somber face to him, and he kissed her again, warily at first, and then with a growing jubilation as he felt her responding. He started to tug her into the livingroom and their feet tangled and she nearly fell. He held her in the circle of his arm while he snapped off the main light switch to darken the living-room except for a small lamp in the corner.

"Tell me you love me," she whispered, and there was a dark anguish in her voice.

"I love you, Senta," he said, and the words tumbled from his lips. "I love you very much."

They were on the couch and he felt the frantic trembling of her body. For a moment a sharp remorse and shame possessed him. Then it was lost in a furious fumbling and twisting of their bodies.

A little before dawn it began to rain. A thin drizzle fell across the evergreens and walks and cast a shimmering mist around the post light near the gate. The first faint trace of daylight cut the rim of the dark night sky. Mark snapped off the post light and walked into the kitchen where Senta had made coffee.

Her cheeks were scrubbed clean of any remaining powder and without a stain of lipstick her lips appeared to be drained of blood. She had brushed back her hair and tied it with a strip of ribbon. He sat down across from her and poured himself a cup of coffee.

"Do you want sugar and cream?" she asked.

"Just a little sugar," he said.

40

They lapsed into silence and drank their coffee slowly. He gave a short and rueful laugh.

"Do you ever see those corny commercials on television?" he asked. "The ones that show the adoring newlyweds saying, 'Good morning, Mr. Jones,' and 'good morning, Mrs. Jones,' and a lot of jazz like that."

"I may have seen them," she said quietly.

"They should have a commercial for us," he said. "Some aspirin company should show us sitting like this, not talking, drinking our coffee with a kind of quiet desperation."

He fell silent again staring into his cup.

"Are you sorry?" he asked.

"I don't know," she said. "I don't really know what I feel."

He twisted restlessly in his chair.

"It's my fault," he said. "I'll assume the full blame if you feel like blaming somebody." He shook his head. "It was kind of a mess anyway," he said. "I guess the excitement and the booze didn't help much. I mean . . ."

"I don't blame you," she said.

"You're not mad?" he asked.

She shook her head slowly. "I'm just confused," she said. "I talked about people in the foreign films doing it when they wanted to do it and afterwards not worrying. But we can't be like that. I don't know why. We go at it like Jerry trying to prove something, or like me, mooning and brooding about whether to or not. We grow up into women like Norma's mother, dreaming of Cary Grant, and men like Jerry's father searching for something we cannot find." She paused and looked at him with a shaken sadness. "And in the end," she said, "a day may even come when we'll no longer remember that it once belonged to love."

Norma entered the kitchen, her face gray and weary in the neon light. Her legs were bare and she pulled at her dress which was wrinkled and showed the lace hem of her slip.

"God, I could use some coffee," she said. "Pour me a cup of black and then let's go. My old lady will kill me."

Senta poured her a cup of steaming coffee from the pot. Norma took the cup and did not sit down but stood blowing across the coffee to cool it. She looked over the rim of the cup at Senta and then at Mark. For the first time she noticed the stained scratch on his cheek. "Some night," she said grimly. "Some night we all had."

She handed the car keys to Mark. "I took them from his pants pocket," she said. "He's out like a dead man. I tried to wake him thinking he might want to drive his little sweetie home," she laughed without mirth. "He opened one eye and looked at me like I was nuts." She took a sip of the coffee and grimaced as the steam curled from the corners of her mouth. "You know he resembled the fish in the picture," she said. "That goddamn fish with the ugly dead eye."

They drove home to Norma's place silently except for Norma's directions to Mark. The three of them sat in the front seat watching the cold day sweep aside the final shadows of night.

Mark parked the car before Norma's small frame bungalow. Norma slipped out of the car, nervously watching the house, and motioned for Senta to hurry. Mark started to get out of the car to take Senta to the door but she caught his arm and shook her head. They stared at each other for a moment and then he looked away. "If I don't get a chance to see you before you leave for school," he said awkwardly, "Good luck to you."

"The same to you," she said. She twisted then to slide her legs from the car. She turned back to him and with a sudden impulsive gesture raised her hands to his cheeks. She held his face for an instant and then kissed him softly on the lips, a sad and fleeting kiss of farewell. Afterwards she left the car and walked quickly toward the house. Norma waited for her on the porch with the door open and they walked inside and the door closed. The gray still silence swept back across the house.

Mark sat there in the car for a long time. A curious weariness possessed him. His head felt heavy and his arms were burdens.

He turned the key, pressed down on the gas, and the car began to move slowly and then more quickly as he gathered speed. He opened the window and let the rush of cool damp morning air strike his face.

the Shearing of Samson

the Shearing of Samson

*I*n a world where uncertainties abound, a man must depend on common sense. Reason is the only weapon with which to combat the hoary superstition and unbridled hysteria of fools. I tried often to explain this to my friend, Louie Anastis, but the man's incapacity to be reasonable merely confirms my observation that he is a lout.

In order that you might better understand the situation, I should first tell you something of Louie and myself. Before his retirement Louie had been a meatman specializing in animals that died natural deaths. He offered these beasts at substantial discounts to any restaurant owner foolish or greedy enough to purchase them. (I do not mention this fact to slander him but because it is the truth.)

As for myself, Alexis Krokas, until my own retirement two years ago I had been the owner of a restaurant. Nothing fancy, you understand, just a small lunchroom with sixteen stools in a factory district that kept me alive for thirty years until it was time to collect my social security.

Then there was Samson. Samson Leventis. He was our

very close friend, a patron of the Parthenon coffeehouse where Louie and I drank mastiha every evening and danced to the bouzouki on Saturday nights. (We managed this feat in spite of Louie's weight and my wretched sciatica.)

Samson was a big man of about forty years, as strong a man as I had ever known. He owned the Zorah Wholesale Produce Company on Halsted Street and could open a crate of produce by shattering the wood with his fist. He had a voice as resonant as a clap of thunder. His clothing consisted mostly of mismatched trousers and coats and he never wore a tie. The most striking thing about him, however, was his thick black hair that he wore so long it concealed most of his ears and curled like a horse's nape over the collar of his shirt.

We were always pleased when Samson joined us and on that night in the spring when he came to our table in the Parthenon, we greeted him warmly.

"Your bottle is empty," Samson said as he sat down. "Waiting too long between bottles causes gas." He called out in his resonant voice and almost instantly old Barba Niko shot out of the shadows with a full bottle of mastiha. Samson filled our glasses.

For a long strange moment afterwards he was silent. Louie and I felt a curious suspense and waited for him to speak.

"My old friends," Samson said finally, "I think for the first time in my barren forty years of life, I am truly in love."

Frankly, I was startled and Louie was stunned. Respecting good sense and reason as I did, I had, of course, remained a bachelor. Louie had been married once for three years and his experience had been a calamity. His wife, a harpy who outweighed him by sixty pounds blacked both his eyes at least once a month and on one frightful occasion even kicked him down a flight of stairs. When he had despaired of ever attaining freedom he received a joyous parole. She deserted him to run away with a Turkish coffee salesman who had the brazen nerve to return to Louie three weeks later and plead with him to take back his wife. Louie hastily put his case in the competent hands of another mutual friend, counselor Pericles Piniotis (the poor devil suffered an untimely death when struck by an ambulance backing up) and achieved a separation. His tragic experience had completely unbalanced him on the subject of women and marriage.

"Well, is nobody going to speak?" Samson cried. "Are you both going to sit there dumb after such news?"

Louis was still so badly shaken he could not answer. I felt it was up to me to observe the amenities. "Congratulations, Samson," I said. "Who is the lucky woman?"

"Not a woman," Samson said fervently. "A goddess."

Louie rose from the table with one hand across his stomach. Samson reached up and pulled him back down. "Sit, old friend, and drink!" he cried. "I know how delighted you must be for me." He caught me watching him and with one of his massive fingers gave me a playful poke in the chest that almost caved in my ribs. "How about it, Alexis?" he laughed. "Does an old bachelor like you know anything about great love?"

"Certainly," I said slightly huffed. "Love is a strong

affection for a member of the opposite sex. Like Dante for Beatrice and Abelard for Heloise." I spoke these references modestly.

"Those are Turkish names to me," Samson shook his head. "I'm talking about real love and not fairy tales."

"Those people were real," I said.

"Is that right?" he asked and his interest was quickened. "That Dinty something or other must be an Irishman, eh?"

"An Italian," I said. "He was a man who loved a woman from the time she was a very young girl. He wrote poetry to her all his life and never said a word to her, never spoke to her."

"The only way," Louie said somberly.

Samson stared at me in disbelief. "Never spoke to her? What kind of nonsense is that? Of course he spoke to her."

"No," I said firmly. "He died without ever speaking a single word to her."

"God bless that man," Louie said.

Samson's cheeks quivered. "Where did you hear that?" he asked.

"That is something I learned back in school."

Samson slammed the table with his fist and made bottles and glasses jump. "That makes me glad I never went beyond the fourth grade!" he cried. "That's sheer nonsense."

"Let me tell you about my wife," Louie said. "My first mistake was talking to her."

"What about the other fellow?" Samson asked me. "That Abe something or other?"

"Abelard," I said. "He was a priest who fell in love with a beautiful girl and ran off with her."

Louie made his cross in dismay.

"That's more like it," Samson gave a long low whistle. "A priest too. That took guts. What happened?"

"Her kinsmen became angry," I said, "and sent some men to take revenge on Abelard. They severed certain parts of his body."

"I knew something terrible would happen," Louie said.

"What parts?" Samson asked. "His legs? Arms? Hands?" I shrugged grimly. A look of horror swept Samson's face.

"The butchers!" he cried in outrage. "The bloody butchers!"

"Violence and women," Louie said bitterly.

"In the end," I said. "Heloise became a nun and Abelard went into a monastery."

"Of course," Samson said with compassion. "What else could the poor devils do?" He sat in somber silence for a moment. "My own beloved is a widow whose husband has been dead five years now," he said gravely. "She moved here from Cleveland six months ago to buy the Sorek Bakery on Harrison Street. She bakes the bread and cakes in the kitchen. That's how I first saw her, her face flushed from the heat of the ovens, and flour smudged across her dark lovely hair. I tell you, old friends, I haven't been the same since." He made a gesture of resignation. "It took a week of going into the store before I mustered up the courage to talk to her. You know I am a pretty rough sort, not much for fancy ways, and enough to scare a real lady when I meet one."

"You are highly regarded," I reassured him and Louie

nodded quickly in agreement. "You can outdance and out-drink any man on the street. All of us respect you."

"Old warriors like yourselves," he said, "but a woman measures things differently. I've been seeing her for two months now. I go and sit with her in the kitchen while she works. Sometimes she lets me take her to dinner. She seems to like me but she also says I lack appreciation of the finer things, that I dress like a bum, and that I look like a shaggy bear with my hair down my neck." He sighed and rose to his feet to leave. "Maybe I could change," he said somberly. "For a woman such as the Widow Delilah, I think I would do anything." He nodded in farewell and walked slowly to the door.

Louie moaned softly. "Delilah!" he said and struck his fist on the table in a puerile imitation of Samson.

"Do you know her?"

"No," he shook his head in distress, "but in the Bible the mighty Samson was destroyed by the wicked Delilah."

"Don't be a fool," I said impatiently. "The names are mere coincidence."

"Any woman is a calamity," Louie said, "but one named Delilah for a man named Samson!" He slapped his cheeks with his palms in despair.

"Louie, listen to me," I said sternly. "Get a grip on your head."

"We must save him," Louie said. "He is too noble a man to be destroyed by an unscrupulous woman." He paused breathing heavily. "I must go to see the Widow."

"Just like that," I laughed wryly. "You will go and see the Widow and ask her not to marry Samson because her name is Delilah. She will throw you on your crooked head."

Louie rose and drew himself to his full, plump and quivering five feet and two inches. "I consider Samson almost a son," he said with emotion. "I must make an effort to save him."

I sighed. I knew the density of that man's head and how impervious he could be to reason. "You will make a mess of this affair," I said. "Since you insist on meddling, I will have to go along and prevent you making a greater fool of yourself than you already are."

Early the next morning Louie and I met at the Sorek Bakery. We stood for a moment outside the window laden with frosted cakes and sugared rolls.

"Now let me do the talking," I warned him. "If you have a comment, make it sensible and brief, if that isn't asking too much."

Louie agreed uneasily. We entered the warm little store scented with the aroma of freshly baked bread. A young slim girl worked behind the counter.

"We have come to call on the Widow Delilah," I said. "We do not wish to interrupt her work but we would be grateful for just a few moments of her time."

The girl retired to the kitchen and returned to motion us around the counter. We walked into the kitchen and met the Widow Delilah.

She was a tall and stately woman in her early thirties. Her face was a flawless ivory oval within a frame of thick black hair gathered into a great bun at the back of her head. Her dark eyes had a startling brightness. There were stains of flour upon the apron which rose and swelled across her majestic breasts.

For a moment I thoroughly appreciated Samson's admiration for her. I gave her a warm smile. When I caught Louie watching me with suspicion, I sobered quickly.

"Widow Delilah," I said politely, "this gentleman is Louie Anastis and I am Alexis Krokas. We are very close friends of Samson Leventis. He has spoken of you with great respect. Since we happened to be passing we thought we would just drop in and introduce ourselves."

"We regard Samson as if he was our son," Louie said ominously.

At the mention of Samson, a deeper pinch of red appeared in the Widow Delilah's already flushed cheeks. "I am pleased to meet you," she said in a husky voice and her lips parted as if they were glistening halves of a ripe plum. She raised the tray of bread and pushed it into the oven with a supple grace. She turned back to us wiping her fingers on a cloth. "I am very fond of Samson," she said.

"Are you going to marry him?" Louie asked in a shrill voice.

A startled confusion swept her cheeks. I gave Louie a hard censuring look and spoke quickly. "Forgive Mr. Anastis," I said. "He cares greatly for Samson and sometimes this causes him to speak bluntly."

She made a gentle gesture of forgiveness. "No apology is necessary," she said. "Your concern for your dear friend speaks well for both of you. You will permit me to speak just as frankly. I am very fond of Samson but I am afraid that I could never marry him."

"Never?" Louie asked eagerly.

"Why?" I asked puzzled. "I don't understand."

"My husband, God bless his departed soul, was a good man," she said quietly. "With his insurance I moved here from Cleveland and bought this store. I am lonely, very lonely sometimes and I would not object to marrying again except that it must be to a man interested in music and art, the things that I am interested in. I am afraid I could not endure a rough and disorderly existence."

"Samson is rough and disorderly, all right," Louie agreed with satisfaction.

"He is a strong man, true," I said. "But he has a purity of spirit as well. He appears unruly and fierce but I have never known him to commit an unkind act against any man or woman."

"He never went beyond the fourth grade," Louie said looking at me indignantly.

"The neighborhood children adore him," I said. "After school they stop by his business for a banana or a peach. You may think, my dear Widow, that you know Samson but until you have seen him teasing and cavorting with a group of delighted children, you cannot know the real man."

"He drinks a great deal," Louie said shrilly. "Two, often three bottles of mastiha a night."

"He is a champion of the weak," I went on swept by growing enthusiasm. "When hoodlums threatened Gavaras, the tailor, and poured acid on his racks of clothing, it was Samson who drove them off Halsted Street. Three men he thrashed that day in a fight that will be remembered for years. They have never dared return."

"He fights a great deal," Louie said loudly and wrung his hands fretfully. "Every weekend, sometimes."

"Let us not forget the baskets he distributes to the needy on Christmas and Thanksgiving," I said. "Many families would go hungry if it were not for Samson."

The Widow Delilah listened in silence. When I paused finally out of breath, she raised her hand in a soft gesture of concession. "I did not know all these things about him," she said, and it was evident she was moved. "He is such a loud and boisterous man, one would never conceive of such goodness and gentleness being a part of him as well."

"Most of the time he is pretty wild," Louie said desperately. "Ask the priest what he thinks of Samson and he will make his cross."

"It speaks well of Samson that he has such loyal friends," she said slowly and nodded gratefully at Louie, "such honest friends willing to admit his faults as well as his virtues. I am sincerely impressed." She offered us her hand in a gracious farewell.

We emerged into the street and Louie trembled in agitation.

"She told us she could never consider Samson," I said to reassure him. "How could I malign him after that rejection? Louie, believe me, I am quite sure this woman was speaking the truth when she told us she would never consider Samson."

55

It was less than a week after our visit to the bakery when we were sitting one evening at our table in the Parthenon. Louie and I had maintained an uneasy truce since speaking to the Widow Delilah. I was sipping my mastiha slowly and scratching my ear when a wild triumphant bellow shattered the darkness of the coffeehouse. Louie was nearly blown off his chair.

The wild bellow rang out again and a big man came stamping between the tables waving his arms like windmills. It was Samson and he came almost at a run to our table. "There you are!" he cried.

The old men from the nearby tables gathered around our own. "Hey, Samson," a graybeard called. "Did you find a pearl in one of your bananas?"

Samson laughed loudest of all. "I don't need a pearl," he cried, "when I have friends such as these two."

"What have we done?" Louie asked fearfully, sensing disaster.

"What have you done?" Samson shouted. "I will tell everyone what you have done! By your loyalty and devotion to me you greatly impressed the Widow Delilah. She regarded me in a new and kinder light. Tonight she consented to be my wife!"

Louie's terrible moan was lost in the roar of approval from the old men around our table but I heard it clearly. Samson started to pull Louie and me from our chairs. "Come with me, old friends," he said. "Tonight I buy drinks for everybody and you will drink the best brandy old Barba Niko has in his cellar."

"You go ahead, Samson," I smiled faintly. "Louie and I will be right along."

He started toward the bar dragging a half dozen of the old men with him. Louie and I were left alone. He stared at me as if I had committed some infamous crime. "You convinced her," he said in a choked voice. "You sealed his doom."

"You are an idiot," I whispered angrily. "A woman isn't convinced by a few words of praise to marry a man unless she intended to marry him all along. She concealed her true feelings. And what if they do marry? The trouble with you, Louie, is that you let one deplorable female sour you on all women. You should have made your wife understand from the beginning that you were the boss."

"Are you mad!" Louie said in a shocked voice. "That monster outweighted me by sixty pounds!"

"Louie," I said more gently, "it depends upon the man. Can you imagine any woman getting the better of a man as courageous and strong as Samson? Can you imagine such an absurdity?" I laughed at how ridiculous the possibility seemed but Louie did not crack even a glimmer of a smile.

"Hey, Alexis! Louie!" Samson shouted from the bar.

I rose from my chair. "Now cheer up," I said to Louie. "Let us go and drink to Samson's nuptials."

"I would rather stop breathing!" Louie said. He rose and fled to the door, waddling slightly under his burden of fat. I went to the bar alone and told Samson that Louie had been overcome by the joy of the announcement and had to leave.

57

We did not see Samson again for almost six weeks following that night. Two weeks after he came to thank us so jubilantly, the Widow Delilah and he were married in Cleveland. Their honeymoon included a week at Niagara Falls. The first awareness we had of their return was when Delilah phoned us at the Parthenon one Friday evening and invited Louie and myself for dinner the following evening. Louie had still not subdued his resentment and apprehension and was reluctant to go until I convinced him it would be a gross affront to Samson.

The next night we dressed in our Sunday suits and walked to the apartment on Blue Island which had been Delilah's before she married. Ignoring Louie's disapproval I carried a small bouquet of flowers for the new bride.

We rang the bell of their apartment. A moment later Samson's voice answered faintly from the mouthpiece beside the mailbox.

"It is Alexis and Louie," I said loudly. "Welcome back, Samson."

The buzzer sounded and I opened the door and started briskly up the stairs. Louie came slowly and heavily behind me. On the third floor Samson stood waiting in the doorway of the apartment.

"Hello, old friend," he said and his voice sounded low and subdued but there was another apartment on the landing and I thought perhaps a neighbor was ill.

"Hello, Samson," I whispered.

There was a single dim light in the hall, a small bulb on the wall near the stairs and I could not see Samson clearly. I noticed with surprise that he wore a white shirt with a tie looped around his throat as if it were a noose. He seemed to be swaying slightly and when I looked down at his feet I did not see the old cracked wide black brogues he had always worn but a glittering pair of two-tone shoes that tapered to an incredibly sharp tip. Samson swung open the door of the apartment and stepped back to allow me to enter. In the bright ceiling light I saw his head for the first time and I almost cried out in shock and consternation.

The great black tangled forest of hair that had curled over his ears and matted around his collar was gone, shorn from his scalp as if he were a sheep, leaving a short bristling stubble over an expanse of pale flesh. For the first time in twenty years I saw his ears and they were crooked and pointed like the ears of a sad dog and skewered at an incredible angle from his head.

Louie, breathing hard from his ascent, stepped in the door and when he saw Samson, he staggered as if he had been dealt a stunning blow.

"Some slight changes," Samson laughed nervously, and his big hand fumbled uneasily at his head as if in futile search for the mop that was no longer there. "Looks neater, eh?" He spoke with the pathetic eagerness of a child wishing to be consoled.

"Certainly, Samson," I said quickly.

Louie could only stare at him in horror. Fortunately, at that moment, Delilah swept down the hall to greet us. She was dressed in a long white gown, her hair coiled in great thick braids about her head. Somehow the sheared scalp of Samson served to accentuate the vitality of her own abundant locks. From her ears hung silver earrings in the shape of slim glistening knives.

"So good to see you, dear friends," she said warmly. "And what lovely flowers? Aren't the flowers lovely, Samson?"

Samson nodded somberly.

"Shall we go in and sit down?" Delilah said. "Dinner will be served in a moment. Samson, put the flowers in water. There is a vase in the kitchen. This way, gentlemen."

Samson started down the hall taking short mincing steps as if he were practicing a dance for the wretched ballet. Louie watched Samson in agony and I had to pull at his arm to follow Delilah.

In a few moments we sat down to dinner at a table covered by a fine lace cloth and set with delicate china and crystal. But in spite of the splendid roast lamb with browned potatoes, the whole meal was a calamitous series of fumblings and admonitions.

"Not that fork, love," Delilah said to Samson, "the other one. Stir with the spoon, love," she said. "Don't hold it as if it is a stein of beer." She spoke gently but with a vein of iron in her voice.

Even Louie and I became apprehensive. Although she did not correct us, she watched us. A number of times I hesitated and let my food grow cold because I could not be sure what bloody piece of silverware to use. Louie seemed to lose control completely once and, missing his mouth with his fork, jabbed a piece of lamb into his cheek.

But I forgot my own discomfort in watching Samson. He sat huddled in misery in his chair, the bright lights burning down upon his bereaved head, not daring to pick up a glass or a fork without receiving an approving nod from Delilah. Every swallow of food seemed to stick somewhere in his throat.

At the end of that cursed meal we were allowed to relax slightly over small cups of sweet coffee. Samson mustered the courage to ask a few questions on his own.

"How are things at the Parthenon, Alexis?"

"Everybody misses you, Samson," I said eagerly. "The dancing is not the same without you. Next Saturday night they are bringing in a new bouzouki player from New York. There will be some wild dancing. Come and join us."

Samson started to nod with enthusiasm and then looked at his wife. Delilah smiled with a slight shrug of regret. "Our Saturday nights are taken for the next six weeks," she said. "Samson and I have reserved tickets on those evenings for the opera."

"The opera!" Louie gasped. "Samson?"

I coughed to cover his confusion. "The opera is very cultural," I said stiffly. "The very best people go to the opera."

Delilah nodded in firm agreement. She shook a gently reproving finger at Louie and myself and with a peremptory movement of her wrist included Samson. "You have all spent far too many nights in the coffeehouse," she said. "There are pleasures far above the bouzouki and bottles of mastiha. There are symphony concerts and the art galleries downtown. I want Samson to learn to appreciate these delights he has been denied up to now. Perhaps the four of us can visit some of these galleries and attend some of the concerts together."

"Certainly," I said, and then I pushed back my chair and rose quickly. "At the moment, however, I have just remembered there is a meeting of our lodge chapter this evening. Please forgive me if I run right off because I am late already."

"I am so sorry you must leave," Delilah said. "I planned for us to listen to some classical records for a while."

Louie rose with a bounce from his chair. "I must go to the meeting too," he said. "Forgive me."

We said goodnight and walked to the door. Samson came behind us. We stood waiting while he hobbled and swayed to join us. We stared at his feet and he smiled uneasily. "They're the latest style," he said. "They're my size too." He looked warily in the direction of the diningroom. "Those damn tips," he whispered. "They're built for men with two toes instead of five." He made a gesture of resignation. "I'll get used to them, someday, I guess."

"If you don't go lame first," Louie said in a choked voice. With a tight forlorn wave of his hand he started heavily down the stairs.

I gave Samson's hand a reassuring squeeze.

"She's a grand girl, Alexis," he said fervently. "She wants what is best for me. I try to go along with her. It's for my own good, you know."

I started down the stairs. Samson hung over the railing. "Say hello to all the boys," he called after me in a plaintive voice. "I'll stop by . . ." there was a wretched pause, ". . . one of these days."

"I'll tell them, Samson," I said, and there was a tightness in my throat. "I'll tell them, old friend."

When I reached the street, Louie waited for me. I expected tearful recriminations but the whole evening had been such a shock, he was apparently having difficulty collecting his senses.

"Just like in the Bible," he said, struggling for breath. "Samson was shorn of his hair by Delilah and lost all his strength. It happened just like in the Bible."

"You are an idiot!" I cried furiously. "Stop talking nonsense! The whole business is sheer coincidence!"

I turned away and Louie reached out and grabbed my arm.

"It will be all right, Alexis, don't worry," he said hoarsely. "Remember what happened when Samson's hair grew back? He pulled down the pillars of the temple and destroyed Delilah and the Philistines." He nodded in a spasm of delight. "It will be all right! Samson will triumph in the end!"

I looked at him in shock. He stood there with his plump cheeks quivering and revelation rising like mist from his pores.

"Louie," I said, and my voice trembled, "Louie . . ." I closed my eyes and had a sudden and bitter vision of those crooked ears and that naked and wretched head. I felt my senses rattled and my reason succumb with a groan.

"Enough, Louie," I spoke in a shaken whisper. "Go to the church and light a candle for Samson. Light one for me too. Ask the priest for a prayer."

"Right!" Louie cried fervently. "At once!"

I turned and started hurriedly away. "Where are you going?" he hollered shrilly.

I did not answer. I assembled my quivering legs and set a furious pace for the Parthenon, staying well beneath the bright beam of the street-lamps.

When reason is staggered by dread and superstition, when sanity is routed by necromancy and spirits from the vasty deep, no recourse remains for a reasonable man but to drown the whole catastrophic dilemma in a bottle of mastiha.

In a world of fools, the lout is king. . . .

the Witness

the Witness

That winter seemed to last forever. At the end of March the ground was still frozen. Walking home from a night shift at the mill, I huddled my head into the collar of my jacket to shelter my cheeks and ears from the biting cold.

By the time I reached home the first traces of daylight had broken the rim of the dark sky. I went in the back door and found Pa in his bathrobe in the kitchen with a pot of fresh coffee brewing on the stove.

In the past weeks he had been having trouble sleeping. Even after taking the pills the doctor had given him, he lay awake through most of the night. Just before dawn he would come quietly downstairs. He would light the oven to warm the kitchen and put on a pot of coffee and wait for me.

I came in cold and tired with the dust of the mill on my cheeks. I wanted only to wash, peek in on my sleeping son and then climb into bed beside my wife, between the sheets that would be warm with her body. But Pa waited for me with a pot of coffee and I had to sit with him for a while.

"Didn't you get any sleep again, Pa?"

He pulled the cord of his robe tighter and turned his face slightly away, because he was no good at deception.

"Better than I have slept in weeks," he said. "Maybe those damn pills are beginning to work."

He poured me a cup of steaming coffee and the sharp aroma pulled at my weariness. "Pa, you made it too strong again," I said, sitting down. "I can tell by the look of it." I was sorry the moment the words were out of my mouth.

"I only put in six scoops," he said. "You told me six scoops was just right."

"Sure, Pa," I said. "Six scoops is right. I just remembered Ethel saying she was going to switch to another brand. Maybe she got one that is stronger."

He walked to the pantry and brought down the canister of coffee. He raised the lid and stared intently at the beans.

"Don't worry about it, Pa," I said. "Sit down and have a cup yourself."

He came to sit down at the table. He dropped two slices of bread into the toaster. Then he raised the pot and poured himself a cup of coffee. His hand trembled slightly because he was old and not well. But his hand still looked big and strong, with the large powerful fingers I remembered as a child. I would get out of school in the afternoon and run to wait for him at the north gate. He would come across the bridge with his crew from the plate mill at the end of the turn. He would see me waiting outside the fence and holler and wave.

He would swing me to his shoulder and the men would laugh and slap my legs. I would ride home high on his back, his hands holding me securely, proud of his strength and his love.

"How did it go last night?" Pa asked as I sipped slowly at the coffee.

"We beat the other two turns by eleven ton," I said.

"No fooling!" His face flushed with pleasure for me. "Who was rolling?"

"The Dutchman," I said. "On all three furnaces."

"He must have been going like hell!" Pa laughed and his pale and tight-fleshed face seemed to flood suddenly with color. Whenever we spoke of the mills he seemed to feel the heat of the furnaces, the glowing slabs bobbing on the rolls.

"You boys still can't touch our record," he said. "I'll never forget that night. Bungo on the furnaces shooting the slabs out like shells from a cannon. Montana on the crane over the hookers. Fuller thinking we were nuts when we gave him the tonnage at four."

He sat up straight in his chair with excitement flashing in his eyes. The doctor did not want him excited, because of his heart and, besides, I had heard the story of that night a hundred times. The stocker with a smashed hand who cried when they took him to the hospital because he didn't want to leave the crew. The way old steel men who had been there swore the crane was a bird snatching up the slabs like a crust of bread. And Pa up and down the length of the mill hustling his crew in a voice that could be heard above the thunder of the roughers and the shrill whistles and bells of the cranes.

". . . And that fool, Barney," Pa was saying, "getting his

hand pulped and refusing to go to the hospital. Even taking a poke with the other hand at one of the plant cops who tried to force him off the line."

"Pa, listen," I said. "We both enjoy talking about the mills, but this morning I'm really beat. I run myself crazy trying to keep up with the records set by my old man." I laughed as I stood up and gave his shoulder a slight punch. "Every few days a damn foreman asks me when you're coming back, so they can start breaking tonnage records again."

He smiled up at me then and I saw the thin clean line of scalp under his thick gray hair. "You're a damn good millman," he said. "Better than I ever was, bigger, and a hell of a lot smarter."

"Sure, Pa," I said. "Go tell that to some of the old-timers and they'll lock you up." I arched my shoulders and stretched. "Let's go up," I said. "Maybe you can get a couple of hours' sleep before the kid gets up."

"You go ahead," he said, "and I'll be along in a minute. I'll just rinse the cups and make the kitchen look nice for Ethel when she comes down."

He stopped me when I reached the stairs. "Don't forget the kid's birthday party," he said, and all the love and devotion he felt for Alex was in his warm wink of anticipation. "Tonight is the night."

I stopped for a moment in Alex's room. He was asleep in his crib, looking like some kind of dark-haired angel. He was quick and bright and a joy to be near. I spoiled him a little, but Pa was worse than me. When Ethel cracked Alex across the behind for something he had done wrong,

Pa left the room because he could not bear to hear the kid cry.

In the bathroom I stripped and shivered as I washed. I went quickly into the bedroom and slid carefully between the sheets. Ethel stirred beside me and I kissed her soft warm cheek. She moved gently against me, warming my body with her own, until I stopped shivering and fell asleep.

Alex woke me a little before one. His habit was to creep softly into the room and climb up on the bed. If this wasn't enough to wake me, he would bring his mouth to my ear and, like a puppy, begin nibbling at my lobe.

There was a joy in waking to the boy's great brown eyes and clean-child smell. I would hug and tickle him till he shrieked in delight.

Afterward I showered and dressed and went downstairs hungry. I kissed Ethel, standing before the stove, and gently stroked her swollen little belly that pressed up against her apron.

"Potato pancakes again?" I said.

"Don't eat them," she said cheerfully.

"Anything else?"

"Eggs."

"I married a cook," I said.

"We get what we deserve," she said. "My mother used to say, Ethel, marry a rich man and keep off your feet."

"You didn't get that little belly standing up," I said. She took a swipe at me with her dish towel and we both laughed.

72

Alex came into the kitchen with cookie crumbs around his mouth and wanted another one. Ethel told him no and I winked at him and slipped him a chocolate chip from the jar. He ran out of the kitchen with his prize.

"It's his birthday," I said.

"You spoil him worse than Pa," she shook her head.

"Where is the old man?"

She motioned toward the back yard and the garage. "With Orchowski," she said quietly.

I sat down at the table and she brought me the potato pancakes and several slices of sharp salami.

"They should play in the house," I said. "Find a place somewhere in the house. That small stove doesn't keep the garage nearly warm enough."

She stared at me silently. I ate slowly, without looking up from my plate. We had covered this same ground often before. I kept bringing it up, even when I knew what she would say.

"Mike," she said wearily, "Mike, what's the use of talking?"

"I know, honey," I said. "But he's not well."

She made a helpless gesture with her hands. In that moment I realized how much of her day was spent in the kitchen cooking for us, washing the dishes, ironing the clothes. The potato pancakes stuck in my throat.

"I know, too," she said, and she spoke softly. "I want to do right, but I want to be fair to Alex, too. Why don't they play in Orchowski's house?"

"You know why," I said. "His son-in-law doesn't like his cigars or his beer."

"They don't have a child like we do," she said. "When they play inside here I can't keep Alex out of their room. Pa hasn't got the heart to lock him out. I don't mind Orchowski's cigars, how bad they smell in the house, but I mind the hollering and the cursing. Honest to God, Mike, you've heard them."

"They're roosters with cut claws now," I said, feeling my cheeks hot. "All they can do is swear and holler."

"I know that," she said patiently. "But curses and hollering are no way to bring up a child." She twisted the dish towel uselessly in her fingers. "This neighborhood is bad enough," she said. "They call it the bush and laugh at the number of bars. When Alex grows older he will need all the strength we can provide him now, all the decency we can give him now."

"All right," I said. "All right, for God's sake, Ethel, let it alone." There was a senseless anger in my throat, because I felt she was right.

She came over and stood for a silent moment beside my chair. I leaned my head against her breast and smelled the flour on her apron.

"Eat," she said gently, and her small soft fingers rubbed my neck in a soothing caress. "Eat your food before it gets cold."

I ate a little more and left the table. I called Alex and got him ready for a walk. He rolled on the floor while I tried to pull on his leggings. I crouched above him and he pressed his tiny hands against my chest, begging me to crush him. My chest dipped against his body and he squealed with fear and delight. I got up and slipped on my jacket and tied a muffler around his throat.

In the yard the ground felt cold and hard beneath my feet. The dark gabled roofs of the mill loomed at the end of the block, throwing a shadow across the houses built closely side by side. The shrill whistle of a crane rang through the clear cold air.

We walked into the garage and Pa and Orchowski were bent over their checkerboard on a small table. Even though the small oil stove in the corner glowed with a steady flame, Pa wore his coat and had a wool scarf wrapped around his throat. Orchowski was dressed in a sweater and jacket and a pilot's cap with the flaps pulled down over his big shapeless ears.

Alex broke from my hand and made a dash for Pa, tumbling into his lap. Orchowski grabbed the board and held it aloft while Pa wrestled with the kid.

"If it ain't the steel man." Orchowski smirked between his pitted checks. He was a bull of an old man, a roller and turn foreman in the old days, and a terror on Saturday nights. "Tell me, steel man," he said. "You still picking up hot slabs with bare hands and swinging on the crane like Tarzan?"

"Leave the boy alone, you bastard," Pa said. "Today they make steel with their heads, not their backs like we used to do."

"I know," Orchowski sneered. "Sure, sure." He scratched his nose. "Play checkers. You're losing and you're trying to turn over the goddamn board."

The kid listened to them intently and I remembered

what Ethel had said. I stood there a moment and shivered in the chill of the garage.

"Why don't you guys play inside?" I burst out. "This place is an icebox."

Orchowski and Pa looked at me. Even Alex stopped wiggling between Pa's legs and stared up at me as if he understood I had said something foolish. Orchowski looked at me with that smirk cracking his lips. Then he turned back to the board and waved impatiently for Pa to move.

Pa kept watching me with concern. "This is fine, Mike." He shook his head at me, slowly at first, then faster and beginning to grin. "Teddy and me like it fine out here."

For a moment Orchowski did not look up. Then he seemed to feel the waiting in the silence and raised his head. Something in Pa's cheeks must have stung him.

"To hell with playing inside," he growled. "Out here we can breathe." Then he slapped his leg with his fist. "You gonna play checkers!" he yelled at Pa. "If you don't make a move I'm gonna go get a goddamn beer!"

"Shut up, you bastard!" Pa cried. "You're a poor loser and a scab!"

I took Alex by the hand and we left the garage. We stood outside in the yard and the shifts had changed and the millmen walked past our fence. Some called greetings to us and some walked tired and silent with their heads bent against the cold. After a while Alex told me he was getting cold and I took him into the house.

After supper that night, while Ethel decorated the cake, I took Alex upstairs and put him into the tub. While I soaped and rinsed him with the spray, Pa sat on the laundry hamper and laughed as he watched him splash. When I lifted him dripping out of the tub, Pa caught him in a big towel and began to rub him gently dry. Then he carried him into the bedroom and they tussled on the bed while Alex screamed.

"I got to dress him, Pa," I said.

"OK," Pa said, and he gave Alex a soft final swat across the fanny. "I'll go down and give Ethel a hand."

I finished dressing Alex and combed his hair. He was a handsome boy with Ethel's fine features. I looked at him with pride and love, thinking of him as a part of my flesh.

Ethel came upstairs and she smelled from the warm and fragrant kitchen. She gave Alex a kiss and waited until he left the room. When she turned to me there were bright spots in her cheeks and a weariness around her mouth.

"Mike," she said, "Pa wants to decorate the dining room and he's making a mess of it. I told him Blanche was bringing a few Japanese lanterns to put over the lights, but he's found some old faded crepe paper in the basement." She paused a moment, with her cheeks pale, and moved her fingers to tug helplessly at her apron. "I hate myself," she said, and she spoke softly, almost in a whisper. "I hate myself every time I complain. He's got no one but us and I want him to know this is his house, too. But I can't help myself." Her eyes became red and I could see her trying hard not to cry.

"I'll tell him," I said. "I'll tell him I want to fix it a certain way."

She shook her head, sorry suddenly that she had come

upstairs, sorry that she had spoken. "Let him alone," she said. "Don't tell him anything. Don't make me feel more ashamed than I am already."

"If he would take a walk," I said, "up to the corner or over to Orchowski's for a half hour, we could finish decorating the way you want." I paused. "Orchowski is coming to the party, isn't he? You told Pa to ask him, didn't you?"

I could see the misery working behind her cheeks. Then it was my turn to feel ashamed, because I was glad she had not invited Orchowski, not for any other reason but that he made Pa seem worse than he was.

We did not speak again. There didn't seem to be anything either of us could say. I started down the stairs and Pa waited for me at the bottom. I muttered something about turning the thermostat higher to warm the house.

"Is Ethel all right?" he asked. I looked away, because he seemed to sense quick when something was wrong.

"She's got a little headache," I said.

He turned away and I looked down on his gray-haired and strong head and the slight slump that rounded his big shoulders.

"If you think Ethel won't be needing me for anything special," he said, "I might take a little walk. Maybe there's something she wants from the store." He had to pass me to reach into the closet for his coat. I looked at him closely, but he only smiled.

"That's OK, Pa," I said. "I'll see if she needs anything." I called up to Ethel and knew that she was standing silently on the landing at the top of the stairs. For a long moment she did not answer, as if she were trying to compose her voice.

"No," she said, "but tell Pa to hurry back. He's sitting next to Alex at the head of the table."

Pa tugged on his coat and walked to the door and closed it behind him.

In about an hour the dozen or so guests for the party had arrived. Ethel's sister, Blanche, had come from the North Side with her husband, who was an insurance executive. He kept walking around sniffing the house. There were a couple of women Ethel had once taught school with and a couple of the turn foremen with their wives. Pa had not come back.

We waited a while longer and Ethel passed around some more cheese and crackers and I opened some more beer. Everybody was getting restless. Alex, becoming impatient, began to whine. I went next door finally, to Max's place, and asked to use their phone. I called the Burley Club, but the bartender hadn't seen Pa. I called Orchowski's brother-in-law's house, but no one answered. On the way back I peered into the garage, but it was dark.

In the house I told Ethel to cut the cake. Alex was crabby and didn't want to blow out the candles. The insurance executive and Blanche had bought him a $22 dump truck and he didn't want to even open the other presents. I was angry and suddenly sick with worry about Pa, thinking something might have happened to him. I went into the kitchen to get another pint of ice cream and when I got back to the dining room everything was strangely quiet.

Pa stood in the front hallway. His hair was mussed, his

collar unbuttoned, and his eyes were bright and glistening in his face. Orchowski, an idiot's grin on his pitted cheeks, stood behind him. The stink of whiskey covered them both like a cloud and fell across them into the room.

I looked once at Ethel and her cheeks were the color of chalk. Pa took a step forward and stumbled and then braced himself against the doorway of the room.

He swept his arm up recklessly in a swing that included everybody in the room. He kept staring at all of us and then he fumbled behind him, catching Orchowski by the coat and tugging him forward.

"I brought my goddamn friend home for the party," Pa said, and the words came slurred and thick from his tongue. "My goddamn friend who worked with me at the plate mill for thirty-six years."

"Thirty-seven years," Orchowski said, swaying and grinning beside him.

Alex yelped then for his grandpa and one of the foremen laughed and walked forward to greet them. Ethel moved and smiled across the pale band of her cheeks. I helped Pa off with his coat and Ethel took Orchowski's jacket, and for a moment in the closet I felt her hand, cold and trembling against my own.

A short while later I got Pa upstairs and helped him undress. He was sobering, his eyes suddenly blurred and melting, and he kept mumbling under his breath. When he was under the covers, I sat down on the edge of the bed near his head. I heard the last of the guests saying good night and the door closed for the last time. Ethel brought the kid upstairs and put him to bed. All the while, the old man lay there with his eyes wide open, staring up at the ceiling.

Ethel came into the room. She stood for just a moment inside the door and then she walked to the bed and leaned down and put her cheek against Pa's cheek.

"It's all right, Pa," she said, and she was crying, the tears running silently down her cheeks. "It's all right and I'm glad you brought Mr. Orchowski."

Pa touched her cheek with his fingers and moved his lips without making any sound. He touched her cheek that was wet with tears, in a kind of caress, and tried to smile to reassure her, and then turned his head helplessly to the wall. I motioned to Ethel to leave the room.

I sat for a while longer beside him. He twisted and threshed beneath the blankets.

"I was drunk," he said. "Honest to God, boy, if I hadn't been loaded I wouldn't have come in like a goddamn fool. I wouldn't have hurt Ethel like that."

"Let it alone, Pa," I said. "What are you making such a big thing of it for? Ethel said it was all right. We were wrong."

But he would not be comforted. He would lie still for a few moments with his eyes closed and I thought he had fallen asleep. Then he seemed to startle awake and his fingers moved in restless tremblings along the spread.

I got scared and left the room and called the doctor. He came and gave Pa a shot. After a while Pa fell asleep, his rough breathing eased and quieted.

It was not very long after that night, only a couple of months later at the beginning of summer, that the old man died. In May we sowed a bed of columbines and Pa talked of seeing them flower and just a few days after that he was dead.

When he died he had been in the hospital two days with a hard and heavy pain in his chest. The second night a blood clot formed and he died in his sleep. We had seen him early in the afternoon of that day, and when they called us back to the hospital, all I remember noticing was how really thin his wrists had become, how slim and pale his strong fingers were.

We buried him three days later. The old rollers and turn foremen who were still alive came, and a bunch of the men from my turn. It rained a little on our way to the cemetery, the drops glistened on the bankings of flowers around the grave. Ethel cried a lot and she was near enough her time for giving birth that I was scared for her and for the baby.

On the way out of the cemetery I saw Orchowski. He was dressed in a baggy gray suit, a stiff collar around his broad throat. I wanted to talk to him a few moments, there beside the old man's grave, but someone took my arm and I lost him.

We stopped on the way home to pick up Alex from Mrs. Feldman, who had looked after him. The rest of the way, Alex between us in the car, Ethel and I didn't speak. I parked the car and carried the kid into the house because of the puddles that still gleamed in the gutters and made small pools along the side of the walks.

The house was damp and quiet. I turned on some lights and put up the heat. Ethel came in behind me and we stood like that for moments, listening as if there were sounds and noises we expected to hear.

"I'm tired," Ethel said. "I've got a headache. I'll get Alex ready for bed and go to bed myself."

"I'll bring him up in a minute," I said. "Let him play for a while."

She stood in the hall and slipped off her coat and the jacket of her suit. The light fell across her body and I could see the great swell of her belly, the slow labored movement of her arms. She saw me watching her and came over and kissed me on the cheek. I held her close in the circle of my arm.

"We tried," she said, and there was a thin tight edge to her voice, and she looked at me out of her weary and swollen eyes. "We did what we could for him, didn't we, Mike? Didn't we?"

I remembered the night of Alex's birthday and the way she cried against the old man's cheek.

"Sure," I said. "Sure, baby, you did."

I sat for a while in the back room watching Alex play with his toy cars on the floor. Outside, the cars passed in the twilight and from the mill I heard the whistling of the slab-mill crane.

I listened to the kid humming a foolish song as he played. I thought suddenly of Ethel dead, someday, like my ma, and me having to live with the kid and his wife.

83

I got up and went into the kitchen. Through the window, night had fallen over the back yard. A few fireflies flickered over the garden. The outline of the garage loomed silent and dark against the lighter sky. I moved to the sink, feeling a tightness breaking in my throat.

When I began to cry, the water running so the kid would not hear, I didn't know for a few crazy moments who I was really crying for—the lost old man or myself.

the Bastards of Thanos

the Bastards of Thanos

The island hospital stood on a small hill overlooking the city, a battered stuccoed two-story building that had endured rain and wind and storm. At the foot of the hill the narrow winding streets teemed with the trade of bazaars, stalls and shops vending spices and silks, cheeses and wines, shrimp and squid. Greek and Jewish and Egyptian merchants haggled and bartered in a babble of harsh and reedy dialects and tongues.

From where Thanos lay in the corner bed of the second floor pauper's ward, he could see the harbor beyond the city, the piers and docks with a few freighters at anchor. He watched the ships make port and sail with the tides and on sharp clear days he marked the flight of gulls that skimmed and soared above the water. At other times he stared at the ceiling above his bed, the surface upon which particles of sun and cloud and the reflections of water shimmered like the billows of the sea itself. During these hours he fashioned his verses, appending each word slowly and arduously, composing another fragment of the long unfinished poem he had begun ten years before. In this way the day would pass until twilight curtained his window. He waited for the lights of the city and the harbor to flicker on proclaiming the beginning of another roisterous night of drinking, gambling and love.

Though there were twenty other occupied beds in his ward, a screen beside his bed and another at the foot shielded him from the remainder of the patients. He heard the clatter of utensils, the skirmishing murmur of voices, the curses and the groans. He inhaled the fetid stench of pus and decay mingled with the antiseptic scents of alcohol, iodine and carbolic acid. But the smells and the sounds of the ward came to him as if from a distance, while in his bed he breathed and endured the cesspool of his own body.

He knew he was dying. The scent of death rose like swamp mist from his pores. His flesh withering on his bones. Even his once strong hands now skewered between fatal illness and age, his fingers brittle twigs needing only a slight jerk to snap them from the frail stem of his wrists.

When he had first been brought to the hospital several months before, the diagnosis had been unanimous and clear. Accepting the coming of his death he fought all efforts to soften his abrasive will, to medicate and console him. He rejected the banal ministrations of the nurses and doctors, scorned their aseptic routine visits that merely served to chart his decline. He vehemently refused the drugs they sought to give him for his pain, unwilling to narcotize the wellsprings from which his poem flowed. He would suffer the pain until he could bear it no longer rather than dull his senses. And even if pain made him howl like a dog he would to the end seek to contour and define even the assembling spectres of darkness and death.

For a little while each morning he had his only visitor, the island Greek priest who came dutifully to attend him on his rounds of the sick. He was a meek and resigned man with a pale, sepulchral face. Fasts and prayer, celibacy and ingratitude, these had drained his spirit and he lived and moved like a shadow drawing what small warmth he could from the candles of his faith.

"How are you today, Thanos?" the priest asked in a frail voice that he tried to make sound vigorous. Thanos knew he regarded the few moments of his visit as a penance.

"Absurdity is still king," Thanos said. "And the poem is the only canon still worthy of faith."

The priest sat down awkwardly in the chair at the screen. He drew his bony legs cloaked in shabby black trousers together and stared at the worn tips of his scuffed shoes. He forced himself to look back at Thanos and managed a wan smile.

"You are looking better today," he said.

"You are a dreadful liar," Thanos said. "Each day all my selfish desires and my absurd vanities decline further into impotence and ugliness. In a short while I will be hollowed out, old as the ages, bare bone and dry brush. And you look about the same."

The priest fumbled his fingers together.

"How is the poem going?" he asked.

"It resembles the old man of the sea," Thanos said. "The Proteus who constantly eludes the grasp, forever changes his shape. But here and there in a word, in a line, it captures pleasure and folly, misfortune and love, vice and elegance, perfidy, betrayal, ineptitude, cunning."

"Is there a place in all of this for God?" the priest said.

"He is there too," Thanos said, "holding aloft the lance and the cup and the Holy Grail. Where he is the water does not flow, love is sterile, crops fail, and animals do not reproduce."

"You build a statue without a pedestal," the priest said patiently. "We are saved by hope and not by memory."

"Spare me your vesicular oblations," Thanos said. "I would not trade a single folly or vice of my life for an eternity of redemption. Your paradise is duller than the landscape of your dismal and surrendered face."

"I have had no reason to laugh in twenty years," the priest sighed. "Even a smile threatens to crack my jaw. Yet although I cannot help my sad face, God may still help you. Believe in him and you may find your burdens lightened."

"I have always believed in the essentials," Thanos said. "Dancing and laughter, yeast and flour, grapes and wine, desire and love, noon and night, words and poems. Why should I forsake them now?"

"There are mysteries we can enter only through faith," the priest said.

"The mystery lies not in the end but in the beginning," Thanos said.

For a moment longer the priest wavered and then he

slowly rose. He bent and raised his small black communion bag.

"I will see you again in the morning," he said. He hesitated and for an instant closed his eyes. When he opened them the lids were heavy with despair. "I pray for a sign," he said slowly. "A sign to prove the power and glory of God. A small miracle to enable you to accept communion."

Thanos uttered a low growl of laughter. "I have swallowed wine by the barrel," he said, "and savored bread by the ovenfull. Your chalice of crumbs and droplets is an abomination."

The priest turned forlornly to leave.

Thanos called after him. The priest turned back.

"Show me a sign of his power and his glory," Thanos said, "and I pledge to take your communion." He grinned a crooked tearing back of flesh from about his hardened and discolored gums. "But if you cannot provide me a sign then you must admit your life has been useless deprivation and waste. We may still be able to provide you a few meagre vices with which to adorn your last years."

The priest coughed a final futile sigh and left.

Thanos did not mind the visits of the priest. He looked forward to them, secretly yearned for them to last longer. They offered him a momentary release from the sputtering and spasms of his organs as they expired.

After the priest had gone, he returned to his poem, forming the words deep in his throat, feeling them hiss and sing through the crumbling canyons of his body. He cherished the words born of sight, smell, touch, taste, hearing and spirit. The fertile element was life, the sterile element was death, and the purifying element was the poem. In the throes of his creation he could still feel the wild strong cries of his soul.

When he needed a respite from the words and lines, he assaulted his memories. He used the myriad events of his life as herbs and potions, sharpening the treasured reveries for battle against the great savage pain he knew would come just before the end. He carefully reviewed the succulent meals he had eaten, the juicy rare meats, the redolent oil and garlic salads, the candled midnight tables of walnuts, cheese and fruit. Upon the parched desert of his palate he trickled once more in fantasy the wines of Bordeaux and Burgundy, Porto and Marsala, still wines and sparkling wines, pale amber champagne and glowing ruby clarets.

He retraced his multifarious journeys across the world. An orphan at six, a seaman at fifteen, fifty years as a poet. He remembered the hundreds of women he had possessed, the countless courtships and consummations. The cycles of desire, the sadness after love, but also, reborn like the phoenix from the ashes, the love after sadness. He tried to extricate the hundreds of shimmering bodies, the lovely faces, knowing that many of them were dead now or grown cold and old with skin like ship's canvas and bodies gnarled and twisted like the trunks and branches of old island trees. But in the fertile valleys of his assignations they would always be young. Brown handsome Polynesians who walked with the pride of Queens. Black wenches in Africa with gleaming flanks and armored breasts. Coal-eyed Jewesses, descended of Bathsheba, like smoke in a man's arms.

Moslem girl children with breasts like plums. Delicate yellow women with the shyness of virgins in their eyes and a whore's skill in the arts of love. He heard them whimpering and shrieking and cursing and giggling and pouting and teasing in the rocking beds of a hundred ports. He fought to hold the vicarious heat of the visions, until finally, shaking and exhausted, he watched them fading into the twilight that engulfed his bed. He cried out then, a bitter lament deep in his body, for the joys he had once savored and would garner no more.

Early one morning in that week he had another visitor. During the night his pains had goaded him almost to the threshold of screams and he had found himself thinking with frenzy of the numbing drugs. The dawn came bleak and pale, the sky a gray shroud against his window. He was staring at the window when a young man entered between the screens around his bed, pausing for a moment as if he were expecting to find someone else.

Thanos turned his head on the pillow and for a time they stared at one another in silence. The youth was tall, with dark eyes and dark hair, dressed in a seaman's jacket, a seaman's knit cap in his hands. Against the sunweathered skin of his cheek the slit of a scar gleamed white.

"Are you Thanos, the poet?" he asked finally. He spoke in a low and earnest voice.

The pain had made Thanos angry and uneasy. "What do you want?" he asked harshly.

"My name is Petros," the young man said. "Petros Potamis. My mother was Magdalina."

"My mother was the Blessed Virgin," Thanos said. "What do you want?"

"Magdalina Potamis of Athens," Petros said tensely. "You were in Athens for a while years ago, weren't you?"

"I have been in fifty countries and in five hundred cities," Thanos said impatiently.

Petros raised his hand, fumbling with his fingers at the scar on his cheek.

"I am your son," he said.

For a startled moment Thanos was silent. Then he began to laugh, a mirthless sniggering from between his lips. Petros stood stolidly until his fit had subsided, until he could hoarsely regain his breath.

"I have no sons or daughters," Thanos said and snorted again. "I have never been chained in marriage and my unions have been unsanctified. You have made a mistake."

"I am your bastard son," the young man said quietly. "My mother was Magdalina Potamis and you knew her in Athens more than twenty years ago. She has married twice, has other children by those husbands, but you are my father. She told me when I was fifteen."

"We all dream of the father," Thanos said. "The comedy begins when we think we have found him."

"My mother told me you had been a sailor," Petros said. "When I was sixteen I went to sea. I asked about you in a score of ports. A few men remembered your drinking and your fighting. Some remembered you shouting out your poems." He gestured with his hands in awkward apology. "I even talked to a few of the women who remembered you."

"You heard about me in some brothel," Thanos cried, "and have come to mock me or to discover if I have an inheritance of treasure to leave. I have nothing but a thousand lines of an unfinished poem that will die soon with me."

Petros fumbled in the pocket of his jacket and brought out a small, worn and faded, paper-covered booklet.

"These are your poems," he said. "I have read them many times. On nights in the Islands of the Indies and on watch in the Galapagos. I have heard them echo in the cries of birds on the shores of Greenland."

"Where did you get the scar?" Thanos asked.

Petros shrugged a slight drawing together of his shoulder, his lips parting in a spare wry admission.

"A fight over a girl in Vera Cruz," he said.

"That could be evidence of my paternity," Thanos said with a snigger.

"My mother gave me the poems," Petros said. "There is one of them, a poem she told me you had written of her. Do you remember?"

"Read it to me," Thanos said.

The young man opened the booklet and began to read in a clear and strong voice.

> A single candle was not needed
> To light our hours close together.
>
> In the distance, the sea,
> The harbor white under the moon.

On the flanks of the mountains,
Wildflowers and the evening star.

Secret places of our heart's love,
Wind and night our bower.

Old and ill I will still remember,
In darkness savor once more the light.

From a yard below the hospital window, a rooster screamed a raucous caw. A dog answered with a short harsh bark. Thanos struggled vainly to separate flowers sundered in the wind of years, petals scattered in the wake of endless tides. With the poem in his hands Petros waited in a silence like the drifting of a ship in a dead still sea, heart and soul ardent for the first quiver of wind.

"I remember," Thanos said. "I remember your mother now." He felt a sliver of pain moving in his blood.

A flame leaped into the youth's dark eyes.

"I have searched for you for six years," he said and his voice trembled. "Searching six years to find a father I had never seen. In Alexandria, two months ago, an old salt you had sailed with told me he had heard you were here. When we anchored yesterday I swept the city for you, wandered all night through the bars that had not seen you in months. Now I have found you and my ship sails in an hour on the tide."

"You found me in time," Thanos said. "A few more days might have been too late."

"I can stay if you want me to stay," Petros said. "I can

jump ship and hide until after she sails. I can stay with you until you are well."

"There is no need of that," Thanos said. "I cannot escape the shipwreck of my body and the end of my voyage is very near."

"I knew I would find you," Petros said. "I swore to my mother I would find you."

"When you see her again, give her a message for me," Thanos said. "Tell her I loved her most of all."

"I will tell her," Petros cried softly. "As God is my judge, I will tell her in just those words."

"I have no possessions to leave you," Thanos said. "Remember these words, my only legacy to you. I was what you are. You will become what I am. Think of those words and you will unravel the way to live."

"I will," Petros said. "I will."

"Hurry now to your ship," Thanos said.

Petros came closer to the bed and knelt quickly. Before Thanos could draw his hand away the son had clasped his palm and gently kissed his stiff dry fingers. The touch of the youth's mouth upon his cold wasted flesh filled him with a strange quivering warmth.

Petros rose and moved toward the opening between the screens. He paused as if to make another plea or effort to remain.

"Don't miss your ship and your mates!" Thanos cried. "A hundred gilded ports are waiting for you, a hundred scented lovely girls. Hurry!"

The young man turned and fled.

Later that morning the priest came on his daily rounds. He stood for a moment uncertainly at the foot of the bed.

"How are you today, Thanos?" he asked.

"Rejoicing," Thanos said, and the words came with a slurring burden from his lips. "Because I am purified by every devilment, sanctified by every depravity, beyond sentiment and fatigue, nearing the realm of pure spirit."

The priest sat wearily down drawing the small black bag close to his feet.

"You are looking better today, Thanos," he said with a frail smile.

Thanos groaned. "Day by day you parrot your miasmic clichés," he said. "A worthy spiritual leader for this parish of drunks, thieves, and syphilitics."

The priest looked submissively at his pale-fingered hands in his lap.

"I had a visitor this morning," Thanos said. "I have been waiting to tell you about him. A bastard son from a far-off port that I did not know I had whelped. He has been searching for me for six years and finds me on the eve of my death. What does St. John say to that?"

The priest rose trembling to his feet and made his cross. "God has heard my prayers," he said in a shaken voice. "To send you a son so close to the end. It is a sign of His power and His glory."

"It was a sign," Thanos said. "A moment of deliverance, an event of revelation."

"God be praised!" the priest cried softly and closed his eyes.

"If there is one son," Thanos said, "how many others

might there be, bastard spawn of my wild beds, born of virgins and whores . . ."

"No!" the priest gasped. "That is not the sign I meant!"

"Think of it!" Thanos cried hoarsely. "Perhaps as many as fifty or more androgynous mongrels of my rampaging journeys, devoted to life and drink and love as I have been, a virile host to carry on after I am gone, hurling my unrepentant seed into myriad races and through endless generations!"

The priest shook his head, a moan of despair falling from his lips. "No," he pleaded. "That is not the meaning."

"That is my meaning," Thanos said.

The priest stood in silence for another moment. His breathing grew calmer slowly, his agitation quieted. The weariness and the resignation settled once more in his pale cheeks. He bent heavily for his small bag and turned slowly to leave.

"I will see you in the morning, Thanos," he said.

"Before you go," Thanos said, "I would like communion."

The priest stared at him numbly.

"Communion, you know, the last rites," Thanos said. "A sign is a sign and I honor my pledges."

For a labored moment longer the priest stared benumbed at Thanos. Then he placed his small bag on the chair. He opened the worn clasp and drew out the golden chalice, the tiny bottle of wine, the container of meagre bread. He worked with slow stiff fumblings, praying under his breath as he blended the wine and the bread.

He brought the chalice to the bed. He dipped the small golden spoon into the wine and bent toward Thanos.

"My God, my God," he whispered, and there were tears in his eyes. "Thy mysterious ways are beyond thy servant's understanding."

Thanos parted his lips and received the tiny spoon of sweet wine and sodden pellet of bread.

After the priest had gone, he lay staring at the ceiling. The arc of day gave way to the shades of dusk. In the twilight the wild rooster screamed again and he heard a savage burst of pain answer in his body.

He fought his fear and panic and slowly, carefully, he cast and forged the words and lines of his poem.

End of Winter

End of Winter

The first snow fell early in November. Almost at once the weather turned cold. Winds howled in the night and shook the house. The oil furnace ran from dark to dawn almost without stopping, but the rooms were still cold. Della and I got up several times during the night to make sure the boys were covered.

In the morning I was the first one up and shaved and woke the boys for school. While they dressed, Della made their lunches and cooked breakfast. We ate together and I left for work about the time the boys headed for the school bus. Della waved to us from the door and the dog next door barked as she always did.

The boys were eight and six years old that winter. Della was pregnant again, we had found out for sure from the doctor just after Labor Day, so we had the winter to go with the baby to be born in the spring.

The pattern of our lives ran much the same as it had for years. In the evening we ate supper and then watched a program on TV—Disneyland or one of the better western stories. I enjoyed them, too. Then, while Della finished the dishes, I put Tom, the six-year-old, to bed. I washed him and tussled with him on the bed. I read him a story and took pleasure in his wonder at the world opening before his eyes. Ralph would come up and wash himself and then the three of us would lie together in the darkness for a few moments recounting the events of the day.

Once a week Della and I went out. A baby sitter came in and we went to a show or a play. Sometimes friends visited us. We drank Martinis or Manhattans and played charades and laughed about many things I could not remember the next day. After they had gone Della and I went to bed and made love.

I know that winter my job in advertising was no more beset by aggravations than it had been in other years. I had been promoted in the summer to brand manager and while it increased my responsibilities it allowed me more freedom as well. I enjoyed my work most of the time and still looked forward to the evenings at home. If the routine of supper and baths and stories weighed sometimes on my back, much more often I was aware of the warmth and laughter.

So in a way I find it hard to understand why that winter, after almost twelve years of marriage, I should have been unfaithful to Della for the first time.

A girl who worked in our offices. Not a girl obviously suited to infidelities the way Norma was, tall and blonde with lithe long legs that gleamed like satin, or elfin-eyed little Dolores who worked in the art department and was always smudged cutely with paint and whispered promises to all the men at the office Christmas party.

Pat had shining black hair the color of Della's. Both had large dark eyes and clear skin. They looked alike except Pat was about 24, the age Della was when we were married.

I remember that afternoon in November when I first suggested to Pat that we have dinner together. She had brought some copy into my office for my approval and stood waiting beside the desk. She had been with the firm about a year and I knew little about her except that she had been married young and then divorced. She had high small breasts and fine ankles. I was conscious of her as attractive, but I swear more than that drew me to her. There was a dream of candlelight and lost springs about her. A fleeting memory of youth as a time of promise. The shadow of some unfathomed sadness about her eyes. Suddenly I felt the stirrings of desire, but not of the flesh alone. A wish to see behind the mask of her face, to share her laughter, and know her well enough to push back the dark errant curl of hair fallen across her forehead. I mentioned dinner to her then, my tone jesting, to provide a retreat if she seemed offended. She was silent for a long moment and I knew she understood the truth. In the way she watched me, coolly appraised me, I knew she had decided to accept.

She met me that night at a small café on the edge of the city. I waited at a table by the window as the snow fell softly across the bare trees in the park across the street. I thought of the years with Della and of the children at home preparing for bed. I thought of the unreality of the moment sitting in a strange café, miles from my house, watching the snow fall and waiting for a strange girl.

When she came to the table she startled me. The snow glistened in her hair and her cheeks were bright, flushed with night and cold.

"I'm late," she said, and her voice was low and husky and her red lips moved easily about her teeth as she spoke.

"I was watching the snow," I said.

I took her coat and saw the soft pale skin of the back of her neck. The waiter came and we ordered wine and then sat watching one another.

"When I walked up," she said, "you looked as if you had forgotten I was coming."

"I was watching the snow," I said, "and fell into some kind of trance."

"Were you hoping I would not come?"

"I'm glad you did."

"I wanted to," she said. "I am not much good at poses. I can't show outrage if I don't feel outrage."

"I guess you thought I was like the rest," I said. "Another married man with problems looking for a young shoulder to cry on."

She watched me silently for a moment.

"I have no problems," I said. "I love my wife and my children. I am not unhappy in my job."

"Then why are you here?" she asked softly.

That stopped me for a moment.

"I don't really know," I said. "I thought of a lot of things when you came into my office today. Maybe I fooled myself. Perhaps I'm here because you are very pretty and I want to touch you."

"That is why I came," she said quietly.

She must have read something in my eyes and she laughed softly.

"I told you I was no good at poses. Does that shock you?"

"A little," I said.

The waiter brought the wine and seemed to give us a look that implied censure. She raised her glass and the wine gleamed red.

"There are many wolves," she said, "behind every office door. They leer and pinch and pat. I don't think you belong among them. You are unaware of all the frantic machinations that go on in the office by men trying to get girls to go to bed."

"How can you be sure I'm not like all the others?" I said.

"I can't be sure," she said. "I think I am right. I think that's why I came. To be made love to by a man who has been faithful to his wife for twelve years is like love-making in a strange land."

So we ate a little and drank more wine and left the café. I sat with her in the front seat of her car with the heater going. We watched the snow falling around us in the deserted park. The scent of wine was about us, aroma of walnuts and richly laden tables. I kissed her lips and tasted ripe sweet fruit.

I touched her body, gently, almost shyly at first and then more rudely as the warmth became flame and still unlike the passion I remembered in the first years with Della. Because even in desire I could not forget those years or the children that waited at home. So there was this sadness as we made love, a sweet and burning sadness, and all the while the snow kept falling out of the darkness.

In the next few months I saw Pat several times a week. I lied to Della of meetings with customers after hours. Of accounts in jeopardy and old college friends in for a few hours between trains. The trust built through our years together helped her believe. After the first night it was easier and I did not think as often of the children.

Pat and I went dancing sometimes in little cafés outside the city and afterwards made love in the car. Other evenings we would spend in her small apartment with the glistening lamps and the Pullman kitchen and the bed that came out of the livingroom wall. We made ham sandwiches, thick with lettuce and tomatoes, and listened to her hi-fi as we ate them and afterwards went to bed. Sometime after midnight I had to get up and dress to leave. She would be warm and sleepy within the sheets and her lips soft as I kissed her goodby. Then I drove through the dark midnight streets to my own dark house. I undressed quietly in the bathroom and looked in on the boys and climbed gently into bed beside Della. She stirred restlessly and moved against me in the bed, warm as Pat had been warm, flesh that was mine where Pat's was borrowed. I would lie awake for a long time listening to the stillness of the house, hearing Della breathing softly in sleep beside me, finally falling asleep myself for a few moments and waking with a start not sure in whose bed I really was.

There were nights when my life of lies and deception bred anger in me at Della and the children. I put the boys brusquely to bed, quick to slap or reprimand. Again there were nights I made love to Pat roughly as if to revenge myself for the injustice upon my family.

The weeks passed into months and the swell of Della's body curved like the arc of the moon. In awareness that her flesh would soon become sluggish and shapeless, she demanded love more fiercely than she had in years. Afterwards we lay together and she would be pleased and feel in some way we were drawing closer together.

"I'm storing up love," she said. "For the baby. I'm taking love from you and holding it for the baby."

I would touch the warm flesh of her throat and stroke the slight swell of her body and feel a strange pain in my chest.

"I am scared about this baby," she said. "I wasn't with the others, but I am scared with this one."

"You will be all right," I said.

"I think I will," she said. "But I am older now. It must be harder when you are thirty-six, not as easy as when you are younger."

"It will be all right," I said.

"Tom was coughing today," she said. "I want to take him to Doctor Vaughn on Friday."

"All right," I said.

"Flora Seaman called today," she said. "They want us

for dinner on Sunday. I called Nora. She can come to stay with the children, if you want to go."

"We'll see," I said.

She rose from the bed and went into the washroom. I watched her, not sure of just what I felt, but something bred of remorse and a shattering of my flesh.

There was a night in March I spent with Pat. She cooked supper for us in her apartment and then barefooted in slacks and a blouse came to lie at my side across the bed. The music from the record player in the corner drew together the small warm room.

"Almost two weeks since you last came," she said. "In a little while you will not come at all."

I touched her ear, the delicate lobe I had gotten to know so well.

"I have been busy," I said. "One of the boys has had a bad cold that keeps hanging on. He waits for me to come home in the evening." I paused for a moment under great tenderness and moved closer to her on the bed. "I miss you when I do not come," I said.

"I miss you too," she said.

We were silent for a while listening to the music.

"I can see it ending," she said. "The little love that kept us warm this winter. There is something sad about love when it is over."

"Why do you say over?" I said. "Nothing is over yet. We will have the spring and the summer. Things will be the same."

She shook her head.

"For a little while you feel a part of you has been lost," she said. "You look into faces on the street to find someone, something that is gone."

"Was your first love like that?"

"That was different," she said. "That hurt in a way terrible to remember. I was seventeen when I married him."

"Where is he now?"

"He is remarried," she said. "To a woman in Dallas who had three children." She laughed softly. "I would tell him he could not accept responsibility, so he showed me. But before that I wrote him long letters. Shameful letters in which I begged him to take me back. He never replied."

She uncoiled off the bed like a cat with warm and supple grace and came to sit on my knees. I put my arms around her waist and felt the warmth of her flesh through the thin cloth of her blouse.

"We should not stay in," she said. "It is not good for you and not good for me. You think of your children and your boy who is waiting for you to come home and I think of my first love and how far he is from me now. We should go somewhere far out of the city and dance and kiss each other in the shadows of a booth and make our love in the car."

"Tuesday night," I said. "Next Tuesday night we will do that. Tuesday night for sure."

I stood up and tucked my shirt in my trousers. She came once more into my arms her dark eyes searching my face.

"In a little while it will be spring," she said. "And in the springs to come will you remember this winter?"

"I will," I said. "I will."

When I got to the street I seemed to smell from far off the faint early scents of spring. The shade of her window was pulled slightly to the side and she stood there with her body shaded against the light. I waved and could not be sure she waved back or not.

When I got home I knew something was wrong. I came in the front door and hung my hat and coat in the hall closet. I saw light in the kitchen and felt a quick sense of dread.

Della sat dressed at the kitchen table. I stood for a moment in the doorway. She knew I was there yet for a long moment she did not look up. I walked to the table and sat down and saw her cheeks pale and still moist and knew she had been crying.

"Wally," she said, and she spoke softly in almost a whisper. "Wally, don't lie to me now. I promise not to cry anymore or become angry. I want to talk to you. I can take almost anything, but don't lie to me now."

I sat there and did not answer.

"There was no meeting tonight," she said. "Lawrence called for you. And then I thought of all the other meetings late at night that you have attended the last few months. All the other things that suddenly fall into place. Then I knew it was a girl."

Her face was naked and her flesh tight across her cheeks.

"Yes," I said. "Tonight and all the other nights. Yes, there is a girl."

She must have expected to hear me say that, but still her face loosened as if the bone beneath the skin had suddenly broken. I was sorry I had not lied, that for a little while I had not indulged all the heated denials.

"Do you want a divorce?" she asked.

"Del," I said. "It was just a girl. I don't want a divorce. It didn't mean that much to me."

"It means that much to me," she said. "Maybe I want the divorce." Her voice rose just a little. "Do you think you are a rooster who can come swaggering back from another hen-house and find everything in order in his own roost?"

"Del," I said.

"Do you think because I'm pregnant now," she said, "and because I have the children that I'm helpless? Do you think you can make me swallow your dirt because I'm helpless? Do you think that?"

"Del," I said. "I don't think that."

"Why?" she said. "I've been sitting here for almost three hours frantically trying to reason why, why? Is it that I'm not a good wife? I don't wash enough clothes or do enough dishes? I make too many demands? I nag too much? I don't keep myself neat? Why?"

"Del," I said, and struggled for the right words. "My God, Del, it was none of these things. Something happened to me. A bad and restless winter. It wasn't right, but it had nothing to do with you."

She laughed a hard little laugh that echoed strangely in the kitchen.

"Has she been the first?" she said. "Has this one been the first or have there been others?"

"I swear the first," I said.

She watched me then.

"What are we going to do?" she said. "What is it you want to do now?"

"I don't know," I said. "I mean there's nothing to be done. I will not see her again. I would have stopped soon anyway. I want you to believe that."

We sat silent for a long time.

"Like a telegram with word someone close has died," she said. "A world suddenly coming apart. I was angry, but I'm not angry now. I am bewildered and confused. I don't know what this means to us." She put her hands across the full swell of her abdomen. "I don't know what this means for this one in my body or for the boys upstairs. I don't know just how to go on or how to turn back. I'm scared and I should still be angry, but I'm only scared and mixed up."

"Del," I said and got up from my chair. I went to her but she shook her head.

"Not now," she said. "Don't touch me yet. I want to believe you. I want you to tell me you still love me and we can go back to the way it was. Then I'm ashamed because it means I have no pride. I'm ashamed and scared and alone."

She stood up and walked out of the kitchen. After a moment I turned off the lights and followed her upstairs.

We undressed in the dark bedroom and did not speak. I went to the bathroom and when I came out she was lying still under the sheets.

I walked to the boys' room across the hall and checked them and came back. I sat on the edge of the bed and moved slowly beneath the sheets careful not to touch her.

"I know what you want," she said softly. "I know what you want."

The house about us was quiet and the room shadowed and still.

"You want the love we had," she said. "You want us young as we used to be."

She moved helplessly beside me and I felt the length of her leg along my own flesh. I took her into my arms and held her tightly against the trembling that swept us both.

There was a sound of coughing from the boys' room. I got out of bed and went to them and Tom coughed again, harshly in the darkness. I pulled his covers about his throat and felt the flesh of his cheek flushed and warm.

I went to the window and closed it a little. The night was cool and all the earth was still. Far off in the dark huge sky the timeless stars glistened.

In that moment a great sadness burned my body.

the Victim

the Victim

Standing in the shadow of a pillar beside the tracks on which the steaming train had just come to a stop, Lenny watched the travelers descend from the coaches and then saw his father. From that distance Charley Hawk did not appear changed at all in the seventeen years since Lenny had last seen him. His hair was white and straight as it had been and he looked just as tall and lean. For a moment he was lost behind a rack of baggage and then he reappeared walking with a grave and unhurried gait up the ramp. As he neared the pillar where Lenny waited, he passed beneath a bright terminal light and for the first time his son saw his face clearly, an ancient mask modeled by death for very old age.

His skin was dark brown and tight across the bone and etched with a web of coarse wrinkles. There were pits at his temples that ran along gullies into the shriveled hollow of his mouth. His nose, always big, loomed now like the great scarred beak of an eagle above the crag of his jaw. He was dressed in a shabby and shapeless gray suit, a heavy cotton shirt buttoned at his throat, a pair of battered work shoes on his feet. His only baggage was a shoe box under his arm, tied with a piece of rope.

Lenny stepped out of the shadow of the pillar. The old man stopped and recognized him without a sign of greeting. Lenny saw that his eyes had not changed, they were still dark and savage and unafraid in the shadow of death.

"How you been, Pa?" Lenny made an effort to smile before the austere face and then abandoned it as useless. The old man answered with a brief, barely visible nod of his head.

"I got my car just outside the station," Lenny said. "I thought we could go to my house first and give you a chance to rest."

"Where's Jim's body?" the old man asked and his voice came in a low harsh rumble from his throat.

Lenny tried to meet his eyes and failing, turned away in irritation to smooth a wrinkle from the sleeve of his dark tailored blue suit. "He's at the Indian Center," he said. "We'll have him cremated in the morning the way you want and you can take his ashes back home."

"Take me to him now," Charley Hawk said.

He turned and began walking again up the ramp. Lenny came a step behind him, sneaking glances at the scarred and stony profile, the erectness of the body attached to the old and withered head. Lenny remembered him back on the Dakota reservation incredibly agile and lithe even in his sixties. He had to be close to ninety now, probably one of the last Sioux alive who could remember having hunted buffalo and fighting in the last Indian Wars against the cavalry. Even now that he showed his age he was still the damn stoic Indian, Lenny thought resentfully, more like the useless legends than the legends themselves.

He swung open the door of the car. The old man bent and moved in without a trace of stiffness. Lenny walked around to the other side and got in behind the wheel. He turned the key and with a roar the motor kicked over.

"Two hundred and sixty horsepower," Lenny could not refrain from a defiant show of pride.

Charley Hawk grunted. They drove in silence for a while. Lenny gave up expecting that the old man would ask any questions.

"He died in the hospital," Lenny said finally. "When I got word he was there I went over with my own Doctor but it was too late. He had been drunk and fallen asleep or passed out in some alley. The rain fell on him most of the night. By the time they found him, he was near frozen. He died a day later and that's when I sent you the wire."

Lenny paused and stared with irritation at the face that might have been chiseled out of stone.

"I know you blame me," he said defiantly. "He was always your favorite. You never cared what happened to me. But there was nothing I could do any more. I got him a job, two, maybe three times in the past three years. He couldn't stay sober long enough to hold one more than a week. I didn't even have to help him that much but I did. He didn't want to help himself."

"I knew he was dead," Charley Hawk said and he spoke quietly as if he were talking to himself. "I had a dream that night. A horde of black-tailed magpies attacked a sick and weak gelding. The gelding screamed. He raised his head straight up. The magpies dug in with their claws, picking at his eyes, gorging upon him until they pulled him down."

"Jesus Christ, Pa," Lenny said impatiently. "Your dreams had nothing to do with it. He drank himself to death and there was nothing anybody could have done to save him."

Charley Hawk was silent for a moment and then he made a harsh spitting sound with his mouth. Lenny gripped the wheel tightly between his fingers and pressed his foot down harder on the gas pedal. The car spurted forward and swept swiftly along between the terminals and factories on either side. The old man stared straight ahead, looking neither to the right or left.

"I had the same beginning as him," Lenny said bitterly. "I grew up on the reservation too. I went to the government school and when the war came I went into the army same as he did. Why couldn't he make his way like I did?" He curled his heavy lips and the words flared from between his teeth. "They told us both, 'Big Chief Wampum good only to sit by his tepee on U.S. 66 selling beads to tourists,' or 'keep whiskey away from an Indian, they go crazy on it,' or 'the only good Indian is a dead Indian.' " He drew a hard shaken breath. "He would always lash back, always fight, and that made them torment him more. I laughed with them and made a place for myself. I got a good job and a nice house and a car and money in the bank."

"He was your brother and of your tribe," Charley Hawk said. "You looked out only for yourself."

"Why not?" Lenny said savagely. "The tribe did nothing for me. It meant nothing to me but poverty and hardship, scrawny cattle and barren land. The dingy shacks and the ceremonies that made no sense and the old men living in the past and the old women always mourning. It was different for you. You remember a time when you were free. But I had nothing and had to fight to make a place for myself in the white man's world. I am respected here. People call me Mr. Carey. They don't even think of me as an Indian anymore."

It came out in the rush of words and the moment he had spoken he clamped his teeth together tightly. They drove along residential streets with well trimmed lawns and lights gleaming in the windows of the houses.

"My house is just a mile or so from here," Lenny said and spoke more softly. "You have known only the reservation and the farm. You don't need anyone close to you. But I want to live like a human being and raise my children and see they have shoes on their feet and hear them laugh when their little bellies are full." He looked into the glass of the windshield, seeing the old man's unmoved cheeks reflected in cold planes and circles.

They rode then in silence until the car pulled up before a two story building on a street of shops. Charley Hawk sat in the car until Lenny had gotten out and came around and opened his door. Then he swung his long legs to the curb and rose swiftly. They walked up to the building entrance and Lenny knocked. After a moment the door was opened by a well-dressed man with a brown glistening face and dark black hair.

"This is my father, Charley Hawk," Lenny said. "This here is Bill Cloud who is in charge of the Indian Center. He has made the arrangements for the services and cremation tomorrow."

Charley Hawk nodded. "Where is my son?" he asked.

"He's in the north parlor," Bill Cloud said. "We laid him out there so that any friends who wished could pass and pay their last respects. We got a couple of nice wreaths already. We notified his American Legion post and although he hasn't been an active member for some years they're going to have a rifle squad at the services tomorrow." He waited smiling for the old man to show some approval and after a moment he looked at Lenny. "That's all right, isn't it?" he asked.

"Why not," Lenny shrugged. "Let them give him the full treatment."

Bill Cloud looked uneasily at Charley Hawk once more and then turned and led them down a narrow hall. From some other part of the building came a loud scatter of voices and a burst of laughter. "Some of the younger boys in the recreation room," Bill Cloud said in apology. "I'll ask them to quiet down."

He paused before the entrance to a room that had long drapes hanging from the walls. A few armchairs and a table with a small potted plant and in the center of the room on a low platform, a square plain casket with a candle burning at the head. Charley Hawk stared for a moment at the casket and started slowly into the room. Lenny moved to follow and the old man looked back at him with eyes like knives.

Lenny faltered. Then he shrugged. "I'll wait for you out in front," he said.

"There is no need to wait," Charley Hawk said. "I will stay here until morning."

"That's all right," Bill Cloud said quickly. "There won't be anybody to bother you. I'll just tell those fellows to quiet down." He moved off down the hallway.

Charley Hawk turned again toward the casket. Lenny watched him for a moment from the doorway. "How can you feel anything?" he called harshly after his father. "How can a Sioux whose heart is made of stone feel anything?" He pulled the door closed behind him.

Charley Hawk stood above the casket. The face that lay within the shapeless folds of white cloth was that of a stranger, the rouged cheeks looking like jagged patches of color on stiff canvas. The body lay stiff and straight in death, the wrists springing like broken stalks from the sleeves of his shiny black suit, and the long brown fingers of his hands folded together over his chest.

The old man tried to remember the face of this son as a young man. His skin had been deep rose-brown, his hair so black a blue sheen glinted over it. He had strong cheekbones and a high arched nose and sinewy arms and strong legs.

Now the face seemed muted and blurred, the mouth marked by dissolute circles, the cheeks and throat more grimly scarred than the old sun dance scars on Charley Hawk's chest. He reached out and smoothed a fold of cloth away from his son's cheek and then sought vainly to rub away the stains of rouge. The flesh felt like coarse stone and would not yield to his touch.

He sat down in a chair beside the casket. He could see his son's face in profile and he studied it in wonder for a long time. He closed his eyes and for a moment he dozed, and in his sleep heard a mare whinny and a stallion answer with a great shrilling. He rose with a start and leaned over the casket. After a moment he spoke with his lips close to his son's face.

"I tell you again, my son," he said. "This land belonged to our people long before the white man came plundering and seeking gold. There was nothing in your blood of which to be ashamed."

He moved away and returned, his eyes holding to the dead man's face as if they were teeth.

"You were impatient with the tribe and the land," he said. "You scorned the plow and the seed. The world of the white men drew you and like your brother you tried to become white yourself. But not all eagles can become ravens."

He stood motionless then for a long time, the flame of the candle sweeping shadows across his face.

"There are no drums to beat for you now, my son," he said. "No painted shields and lances to wave for you in the air. No songs to be sung at your pyre."

He sat down again beside the casket. He stared at the great veins in the backs of his hands, dark and hard, smoke-dried like old meat.

"If I had been born thirty years before," he said, "and

you had been born my son then, you might have become a warrior, one of the great men of the tribes like Black Moon or Crow King or Spotted Eagle. You might have ridden a fine buckskin yearling and followed the winter frost cloud of a buffalo herd."

He leaned his back against the wood of the chair. He stared at the white cold ceiling overhead.

"You might have known the scent of sweetgrass and sage burning in the council lodge," he said. "You might have hunted the swift antelope showing their white rumps in flight and heard the fall whistle of the mating elk. You might have taken as a wife a daughter of a chief with bracelets of copper and silver on her strong arms. She would have borne you many sons who would have grown up with deep chests and sinewy arms and they would have ridden the prairies at your side. All this you might have known."

He rose then and slowly went to open the small box he had carried in with him. There were ashes in the box and a long glistening eagle feather and a slim handled knife. He scattered the ashes across his own head and shoulders and he carefully placed the eagle feather beside his son's head so that it rose like a warrior's plume from his hair.

He picked up the knife and ran the blade around his left forefinger until it drew a thin line of blood. Then he sat down and put his hands over his son's folded hands. He leaned his head against the rim of the casket and closed his eyes. He began to chant softly, a chant that became a low terrible wail.

Chrisoula

Chrisoula

She could not live the remainder of her life in mourning. For a while she would wear her widow's black raiment and grieve for her man murdered in the summer of his life. When she could no longer bear her cold and solitary bed, she would find another man to love her, a man, perhaps, she too might love. That was the way of the flesh and of life. But for as long as she lived, Petros would always remain, for her, the first of men and the best.

Yes, he was a man who could not tell a tale without dazzling lies. He held before him the vision of fair-seeming but false glories. He scorned that which was seemly and good, and blindly pursued that which was graceless and evil.

But he was also tall, raven-haired, with black eyes that gleamed like those of a gypsy. His lips glistened as if he had just bitten into a ripe, sweet plum. She had only to look at his lips and be filled with desire. His arms and shoulders were as powerful as a gymnast's and yet his waist was lean as that of a boy. To watch him enter or leave a room was a delight. He walked in a lithe, strong stride as if he were on his way to or returning from a festival.

He was a man of swift movement and strong beat, untamed and reckless and unafraid of anything on earth. He courted Chrisoula as a princess might be courted with a radiant grace. He brought her flowers, sang to her at night under her window while her sisters giggled and peeked from behind the blinds. He would eat dinner with her family on Sunday evenings and to her father's distress would jump up several times during the meal to regale them with a story that he acted out with fervence and skill. There were times he seemed a marvelous child adrift in a world of adults and at other moments, when they were alone, a mature man. He was twenty-five when they married in the autumn of that year and Chrisoula was twenty-two.

On the night before the wedding, her father took Chrisoula into the basement of their house, away from the ears of her mother and sisters.

"You love this man, I know," her father said. "You love deep in your blood in the way of our people. I am resigned to this love and understand nothing I say or do can spare you the grief you will endure. Go then and marry with my blessing. But when you take this man as your husband, forsake all thought of serenity, a peaceful house, a consoling old age."

"I love him, papa," Chrisoula said. "I will endure what must be endured."

"You will endure," her father said sadly, "but you cannot imagine how much. This man lives out of his time and his place. Centuries have passed him by. The stars and the rivers and the mountains call him back."

"I will help him, papa," she said. "My love will protect him from harm."

"It is not enough," he shook his head wearily. "One can more easily destroy than save with love."

He reached out to her then and with his fingers touched her cheek in a mute and consoling caress.

For a little while that autumn, Petros and Chrisoula lived as God must have wished men and women to live. They made a refuge and a haven of their three small rooms that looked out upon the street of shabby tenements and dingy stores. When they ventured out to shop for food and wine or to walk in the last fragrant twilights of October, people moved like shadows about them and sounds seemed to come from a distant world.

At night they lay naked together, watching from their bedroom window the sky like a moon-splashed sea and the stars glittering rings and circles of light.

"Do you know why I love you?" Petros asked.

"Because I am a peach and a pomegranate," she said. "Comely as the bride of Solomon with breasts that ravish your eyes."

"You are an insufferable woman!" he laughed. "You take a man's songs from his mouth before they are spoken!"

"I only tell you what you have told me before," she said and kissed him.

"That was before," he said. "Each day and night I love

you differently. I savor your face when you laugh, cry out, or in your moments of melancholy."

"My darling," she whispered.

"Listen to me," he said, and his voice trembled. "I have seen many marvelous sights on this earth, a storm in the mountains, a ship under sail on an azure sea, a bride dancing at her wedding. But the naked loveliness of my beloved is the supreme sight of all."

She reveled in his endearments, delighted to feel him asleep beside her, their legs side by side, her toes touching his ankle. Above all she loved the moments of their passion, his fingers pressing her shoulders, his lips curling upon her breath. She felt then the shudders which began as ripples and rolled into great waves across her body. It was as if they rode the crest of a wild sea, their bed a tossing ship, the ceiling of their room a boundless sky.

Sometimes, afterwards, she would cry, the tears rolling slowly down her cheeks. He would hold her tightly and kiss her eyes.

"You foolish little girl," he said. "When you should be the happiest after we love, you cry."

"You are the foolish one if you do not understand why I cry," she said. "After a moment so exquisite I cannot help but think of us as old, someday emptied of youth and passion, withered leaves falling to the earth to die."

"We mustn't waste time brooding about death," he said. "There is too much life to be lived." He leaped from the bed to stand like a naked young god above her.

"But if by some quirk or mischance I should die," he said gravely. "Ornament my body with basil and mint in the way my mother adorned the corpse of my father, and scatter the petals of flowers across my eyes . . ."

"Petros!" she cried, and her blood ran cold. "Petros, stop!"

"Make the house rock with your widow's grief for a while," he laughed, "and then find a hardy man for your lonely bed."

"Damn you, stop! Damn you, damn you, stop!"

He came quickly to kneel beside her on the bed.

"I am sorry," he said, and he was shaken with remorse. "I was only teasing. I am sorry, my beloved, forgive me." He kissed her temples and kissed her eyes. "Love is stronger than death," he whispered, "and our love will live forever, setting eternity ablaze with its burning song."

She took him then into her arms, holding him as a mother holds a child unaware of the grim shades of life. She held him until he had fallen asleep, her naked breasts a plumed pillow for his fine dark hair.

When they married, Petros was working as a bread truck driver, one of many jobs he had worked at through the last few years. He had been a bartender, counterman, had driven a produce truck, and loaded bags of potatoes at the market. After their marriage none of these jobs seemed to satisfy him. He was conscious suddenly of the responsibility of marriage. Chrisoula's father reluctantly offered him a junior partnership in his grocery business, but Petros scorned the offer as a gratuity. He grew vexed and sullen.

"There are many women on this street whose bodies

have aged through too much work and too many children," he said. "They might have been lovely once but the years have hollowed them out. They can no longer laugh or sing. I will turn the saints out of heaven before I let that happen to you."

"I am young and strong," she said. "Don't worry about me."

"On my route in the stores where I deliver bread," he said, "I see the wives of other men in fine clothing, driving fine cars. Why should my wife have less than these women? Am I less a man than their men?"

"I have you," she tried to comfort him. "Those wealthy women would trade all their possessions and their sad husbands for someone like you."

He shook his head impatiently. "I am your husband now," he said. "I must look after you, provide you the things which people respect."

"People will respect us if we are true and live well in the eyes of God," she said.

"Chrisoula, will you listen!" he cried. "It is not what you are willing to settle for, but what I feel you should have."

"Petros, be patient," she pleaded. "We have our love, the days and nights we share together. The rest will come. Be patient, my darling."

"To hell with patience," he said, and closed his heart like a stone against her.

For several weeks afterwards, Petros brooded. He was late coming home from work and told her he had been looking for other employment. She knew by his breath and the sodden glint in his eye that he had spent the time in the taverns.

There was an evening in November, a sharp cold night, when she heard him shouting from the street below. She opened the window, shivering slightly in the cold air, and saw him standing on the sidewalk below with a man she recognized as Antonio Gallos.

"We are coming up!" he cried. "I am bringing Mr. Gallos up! Take out the glasses and the wine!"

He tugged Gallos by the arm and they entered the doorway. Chrisoula closed the window confused and suddenly frightened.

Antonio Gallos was well known in their neighborhood. As a child she had heard her father curse after Gallos had driven past them in his great glittering car. He was a fat, heavy-jowled man who wore diamonds on his fingers, and expensive tailored clothes wasted on his obese frame. He owned a candle company and a bakery. He owned, as well, three gambling parlors packed all day with men wagering on the horses, dice and cards. The candle company and bakery he maintained as a facade of respectability which fooled no one since they all knew the gambling parlors provided him his wealth.

She took off her apron, started nervously to smooth back her hair and then angrily stopped. She walked to the door just as it burst open and Petros entered.

"Come in, come in, Mr. Gallos!" Petros motioned him over the threshold. Gallos entered wearing a fine black cashmere coat and a white silk scarf, in sharp contrast to Petros' jacket and cap.

"This is my wife, Soula," Petros said. "I told you she was a beauty, didn't I? Soula, this is Mr. Gallos."

Gallos stood staring at her, blinking slightly in approval. The skin of his face was sallow, his nose long and thin, his lips meager and colorless.

"Please come in," Soula said and avoided asking for his coat.

"Give me your coat, Mr. Gallos," Petros said and glared at her.

Gallos drew off his gloves slowly, and his hands were small, his fingers blunt and unsightly. On two fingers of each hand he wore sparkling diamonds.

Petros helped him off with his coat and Gallos walked into the small parlor and sat down heavily on the faded cushions of the couch. He drew his shiny pointed shoes back carefully from a threadbare section of carpet.

"I have brought Mr. Gallos home to meet you and to have a glass of wine," Petros said, a sullen anger beginning to stir in his voice. "Mr. Gallos has honored us by offering me a fine postion."

"I'm sorry, there is no wine left," Chrisoula said. "We finished the bottle last night at dinner."

"No wine!" Petros cried in dismay. He made a gesture of apology to Gallos. "A house without wine is a body without blood. I will go downstairs and buy some."

"Never mind, Petros," Gallos made a small delicate shrug of his shoulders. "We can have a glass of wine together some other time."

"I beg your pardon, Mr. Gallos," Petros said, his voice rigid with pride. "In your house and in your business, you command and I will obey. In my house, as my guest, I will command. You will please wait just a few moments. Soula will keep you company. I will go just a few doors down the street and return instantly."

Then he was gone, rocking the door closed behind him, his feet beating a flurried descent.

For a long, stiff interval the room was silent.

"The weather seems to be turning colder," Gallos said finally, and looked down at his shoes.

"Yes," Chrisoula said.

He nodded. "To be expected, of course, this time of year."

"Mr. Gallos," Chrisoula said. "What work will Petros be doing for you?"

He brushed a speck of lint from his trousers and frowned as he looked toward the window. "A number of duties relating to my business," he said.

"Which business, Mr. Gallos?" she asked quietly.

He looked at her startled and blinked. A slight, uneasy smile trembled the thin flap of his upper lip.

"You are a handsome woman, Mrs. Zervas," he said, "and a blunt one too. I admire that quality in a woman. My blessed mother was like that, God rest her departed soul. Kept my poor father off balance all his life." He stared down at the rings on his fingers. "It is well known that I operate several gambling rooms in this neighborhood. But I maintain them as honestly as I can. I provide people a place for the excitement they find in gambling.

This Christmas I will have been in business here forty years." He sighed. "Frankly, I am tired. After all, I am not as young as I used to be. And I find fewer and fewer men I can trust. Would you believe, Mrs. Zervas, that everyone steals from me? My managers and dealers and ticket writers and runners." He fumbled his fingers nervously together in his lap. "There are those who say that I operate outside the law. That is completely false! I am in perfect harmony with the law. I have one captain, three lieutenants, six sergeants on my payroll. Every Christmas more than a hundred policemen receive baskets from me with turkey, ham, cheese and fruit, and bottles of good wine. Their families enjoy a pleasanter Christmas because of my generosity."

"Forgive me, Mr. Gallos," Chrisoula said. "What role will Petros play in all of this activity?"

He did not answer for a moment. He stared anxiously at the door, as if eager for Petros to return. He looked back to Chrisoula.

"I have been watching Petros for quite a while," he said earnestly. "I admire his energy and his courage. He is bright and quick and people are drawn to him. I believe he is honest. What I wish him to do for me is to keep a close check on all phases of my business. Collect the monies from my managers, keep an eye on my dealers and runners. Satisfy my customers that they are being treated honestly. You need not worry about Petros if he works with me. I will look after him and he can go far with me."

"We may not wish to go your way," she said.

He nodded slowly and then sighed. "Long ago when I

was young," he said, "I tried to be fair and good and make a living for myself in some conventional occupation. But I was ugly, sin enough, and worse than that, innocent. Yes, I admit my ugliness and my innocence. You see I can speak as bluntly as you. But I quickly learned that society is composed of thieves. Whether in mahogany-paneled offices on La Salle Street or in my gambling rooms, all steal in one way or another from others. He who steals the most achieves the greatest wealth and success."

"That is not true, Mr. Gallos."

"Please, Mrs. Zervas," he cut her off with a quick nervous flutter of his fingers. "Allow me to finish, I beg you. Petros will be back in a moment and I may not have another chance to explain this to you." He rubbed his palm gently in a caress across the rings on his other hand. "I want Petros to prevent others from stealing what is mine. It is as simple as that. In return, I will pay him well, and, who knows. I am childless and not well. After I am gone the business must belong to someone."

"No," she said, and felt a sliver of fear pierce her heart. "No."

"Yes!" he said, and for the first time a force and conviction entered his voice. "Yes! In this life there are only victims and masters. Petros will always remain a victim driving a bread truck."

At the bottom of the stairs the street door closed with a bang. Gallos jumped as if the noise had startled him.

"Remember what I say," he spoke in a hurried whisper. "Don't make your husband a wound to fit another man's arrows . . . help him fashion arrows of his own."

The door opened and Petros entered carrying a full case of wine on his shoulder. With ease he swung the case to the table. He reached in and pulled out two bottles of wine and held them high over his head. "Wine for my darling and for my new employer!" he cried. "Soula, the glasses!" His voice trembled with excitement. "The glasses so we can drink to the future!"

Chrisoula rose and started to the kitchen for the glasses, fighting the despair that curled like a black, long snake in her body.

For the next few months, through the coldest part of winter, Petros supervised the handbooks for Gallos. He made sure they functioned in accord with Gallos' wishes. In return for this protection, Gallos was generous. Petros brought home more money each week than he ordinarily had earned in a month of work. After a few futile efforts to convince him that what he was doing was wrong, Chrisoula gave up and kept silent. And each week the money increased. Petros bought new suits for himself and new dresses for Chrisoula which she secretly returned.

When she refused to move from their small apartment to larger, more lavish quarters, Petros had all the old furniture carted away and replaced it with new chairs, bureaus, a table and a large, gaudy and expensive couch. One afternoon he drove home in a new car and she rode with him in it while he chattered as excitedly as a child. All this time she was gripped by a premonition of catastrophe.

Sometimes lying beside him at night, watching the pale winter moonlight sweep the ceiling of their room, feeling his body warm and quiet against her flesh, she rested within the serenity and love they had in the early months of their marriage. But in the morning she woke to another day filled with foreboding.

For all her despair, Petros was happier than he had been in years. Each triumph fed his vanity and his pride. Because of his energy and effort, Gallos prospered, and opened two additional handbooks, the first such expansion in more than twenty years. Petros tasted the respect and envy of other men and found it a savory wine. They called him the young crown prince and it was rumored that Gallos was as fond of him as if Petros were his son.

The marauders came from across the city, lean, hard men with the souls of maggots. They had heard of Gallos expanding his gambling and came for his spoils. They bombed one of his handbooks, and, in terror, Gallos wanted to give up. In his old age he feared for his useless life. But Petros scorned their threats. When two of them came to Gallos to present their ultimatum, they found Petros waiting for them instead. He took on the two of them, laughing with excitement as his powerful arms beat them into a bruised and bloody retreat. He regarded the fight as part of a jubilant game, a game in which the contestants were honorable men.

That night flushed with the heat of his triumph, he celebrated in a circle of admiring, shouting men while Gallos ordered case after case of wine for the hordes to toast the young prince of his realm.

Chrisoula waited for him to come home. She walked

through the rooms, her shadow rising and falling in frantic sweepings along the walls. She marked each passing minute as if it were an hour. When she could endure waiting no longer, she went down to the street.

The night was bleak and cold, a smell of snow riding the air. She followed his triumphant trail from one tavern to another. In the last one, they told her he had left a few moments before to go home. He had convinced the neighborhood florist who had been drinking in the tavern to unlock his shop a few doors away so he could assemble a cluster of bright flowers to carry home to his wife.

She hurried the blocks back home and at the corner of their street, she saw him almost before the entrance to their door. She cried out his name, her voice shrill and clear across the frosted and silent street. He turned and waved the massive bouquet of flowers. Her heart flew out to him and she started to run to his arms.

She saw the lights of a parked car suddenly flash on, veiling Petros in a strange luminous mist. As he turned around, the car surged forward. A fearful cry from Chrisoula's throat was lost in the stuttering thunder of the shots.

For a moment Petros seemed to leap off the street, a great spring to carry him over the roofs of the buildings, a stunning and impossible effort to escape. Then, as if his heart had burst, he fell back to the earth and the flowers scattered in the wild wind of his wake.

When she reached his body and saw the blood, she screamed a great tearing apart of her flesh. She fell across his chest and kissed his mute limp mouth. Shouts and lights broke the night around her. Two men sought to pull her away and with her fingers curled like claws she went like a hawk for their eyes.

They let her alone. She knelt beside him and stared at his face, startled and shattered in death. A few flakes of snow fell and glistened on his temples and in his hair. She picked up petals of the strewn flowers and put them gently on his lips and over his eyes. The snow fell on the flowers and gave his face a misted and serene beauty.

Only when her father came would she allow Petros to be taken from her, to be washed and anointed and dressed. And in the old ways of their people to be decked with basil and mint.

In the sunless and damp room of the dead, the old women mourning and whispering like black crows, she knew he was gone. At the cemetery with the people standing like faceless statues around his grave and the cry of a bird falling shrilly from the sky, she knew he was gone. And for weeks afterwards in her solitary bed, her breasts and loins chilled as if death had become her lover, she knew Petros was gone and would never return.

The weeks passed into months and then the winter was over. The first traces of new green grass appeared in the vacant lots. A single tree, stunted in the shadow of bricks and mortar, sprouted a few fragile buds. In the twilight the air was shaken with fragrant wind from warmer land.

Each day the sun grew stronger. From the dismal buildings the old men emerged like moles to sit on their stone steps blinking in the glaring light. Children cast off the garments of winter and shrieked joyously in play.

With the renewal of spring, Chrisoula felt the resurgence of her body. She walked the sunlit streets conscious of the bold staring eyes of men. At night she lay restlessly in her solitary bed, watching the haunting waves of the moon, hearing the husky laughter of couples passing in the darkness of the street below her window. Spires and towers moved through her fantasies. When she slept fitfully and wakened, the pillow which had been beneath her head was clasped tightly against her breasts and loins.

She came to understand in the lonely passage of those long spring nights that the time of love was brief and that vows of eternal fidelity faltered before the yearnings of her body. There was nothing the dead could offer the living but lament.

So she cried softly for Petros. Then she slept and dreamed of the wild laughing lover she would someday bring to her cold and dormant bed.

Homecoming

Homecoming

On the way into the city, Alex picked up a hitchhiker, a seedy youth about nineteen or twenty with long, thick hair and shaggy sideburns. He wore a faded leather jacket and carried a worn duffel bag.

They rode in silence for a while, Alex thinking about seeing Miriam again after almost three years. The youth stared out of the window. They entered the perimeter of the city, the highway burgeoning through a landscape of small shacks and stunted houses, wrecked and partially dismantled cars littering the weed-tangled yards.

"You live in Chicago?" Alex asked.

The youth shook his head.

"I'm catching a bus for San Francisco," he said.

"Got a job there?"

The youth was silent for a moment and then he turned and looked at Alex.

"I'm 1 A," he said. "I'm going to refuse induction. I heard the judges in Frisco give lighter jail sentences."

The words were spoken with such finality there seemed

nothing to add. Alex nodded and didn't speak. The houses began to cluster more thickly on the land, old frame dwellings with decrepit, unpainted porches. Here and there a few solitary trees with tinted leaves formed a bright fresco of autumn.

"I was in Korea," Alex said. "No war makes sense. But I wouldn't have had the guts then to do what you're doing now."

"If you had," the youth spoke quietly without turning his head, "maybe we wouldn't have to go through this now."

"Maybe you're right," Alex shrugged wryly. "Seems so long ago I can't remember what I felt like then."

They rode in silence again along one of the expressways tracking into the heart of the city. The roofs of buildings gleamed below, their windows masked and blurred, concealing the men and women who lived inside. Only when they descended a ramp to the street did the inhabitants suddenly become visible. Alex dropped the youth a block from the bus depot.

"Good luck," Alex said.

"Thanks," the youth said. "Thanks for the lift too."

The light changed and Alex drove off. In the rearview mirror he saw the youth crossing the street against the light, the duffel bag bouncing against his leg as he walked with a certain and defiant stride.

The midday sun, waning with the glitter of October, shone across the expanse of Grant Park as he turned onto the outer drive and followed the curve of the lake. A boy and girl sat close together on one of the slopes of grass.

He recalled the spring morning three years before when he and Miriam had lain against one of the same slopes, feeling the scales of winter peeling from their flesh. In the jubilation of the season and the sun they had danced a wild abandoned little dance together, an old man on a bench a hundred feet away staring at them as if they were mad.

Afterwards Alex kissed her and tasted on her lips the sweetness of the orange juice they had drunk a while before. Then, wordlessly, possessed by desire, they had hurried to the car and driven to her apartment a few miles away to make love.

The white caps of breakers rode the waves toward the shore. He felt a curious surge of hope, unlike the resignation he had endured driving across the country. He knew even before he had started out the probable futility of any effort to recover the love he and Miriam once had. But he had come doggedly anyway, driving instead of flying, preparing his words and at the same time perhaps delaying the foundering of the dream. Now, suddenly, between the surf and the sky he was no longer convinced he would fail.

Miriam had moved from her apartment to another place but she still worked for the same agency. He had phoned her from California on the day he left but when the operator rang her department he panicked and hung up, afraid she'd tell him not to come.

He pulled over to a wayside telephone and got out and dialed the number. A woman in her department told him Miriam was still out to lunch. He left no message and hung up.

He thought of waiting downtown on the chance she

might leave work to see him before the end of the day. He knew that was unlikely and then, despondently, he decided to go and see his mother.

He followed the drive south and turned off at 67th Street. A few blocks later he pulled up before his sister and brother-in-law's house, a narrow, high stucco dwelling, a few sparse evergreens before the porch, the grass in need of cutting. As he emerged from the car a cluster of small black children on the porch next door fell silent and stared somberly at him. He waved to them, smiling, and one boy of about four started to wave back. An older girl snapped him as immobile as a tiny ebony statue.

He crossed the walk and ascended the stairs, bracing himself for the meeting with his mother whom he had not seen in the three years since his departure. In one of the few letters exchanged with his sister, she had told him the old lady was failing, senility, illness and old age combining to push her closer to death. In the last letter his mother had written him herself he could barely decipher her illegible scrawl.

He stood for a moment before the front door, seeing through the sheer curtains into the hallway and the small kitchen beyond. He recognized his mother's short, stocky body sitting at the kitchen table, bent over tea or a bowl of soup. He felt a strange cracking of the shell of the past, remembering all the times he had stood before this door and in the instant before inserting his key in the lock, seeing her at the table in the kitchen.

He rang the bell. He watched her head turn slightly, and then, slowly, heavily, she rose. She came shuffling toward the door, one shoulder lowered slightly because of the arthritis in her arm. He saw her fingers fumbling to pull aside the curtain and he bent toward the rim of the glass. She could not discern him clearly, continuing to peer fearfully through the window.

"Mama," he said loudly. "It's Alex. Alex."

He saw the tremor sweep her cheeks and she flung both hands toward the knob of the door. She struggled and tugged, unable to coordinate her fingers. He heard her crying out his name and, finally, she jerked the door open. For one spectral and terrible moment he saw how she had changed. Then he bent and embraced her, assailed by the familiar scents of incense, rosewater, sweat, and that peculiar, indefinable odor he remembered from childhood, an odor of spice locked in a container a long time and when finally opened, mingling pungence with a thin asthenic staleness.

They sat in the small parlor, side by side on the old worn sofa, the afternoon sun raising a wraithlike mist in the corners of the room. She clutched one of his hands between her thin-fleshed fingers. Whenever he looked at the ravages of illness and age marking her face he felt compelled to turn away.

"Your sister and Chester are both gone in the morning before I wake up," she said in a soft plaintive voice. "Before I open my eyes I hear the emptiness of the house and know I got to be alone all the day till they come home at night. I pray to God, then, for him to let me die."

"Don't you have coffee with the neighbors anymore? What about Mrs. Garfakis?"

"She moved with her son to Glencoe," his mother said. "A lot of people moving now. The Felton house next door was sold to colored about six months ago. Pretty soon the whole neighborhood will be black."

"They've got to live someplace."

"They don't bother me," his mother said. "They wouldn't bother with an old lady. I stay in the house and keep the doors locked. But Chester worries about your sister." She paused and stared at him with her eyes frightened and pleading for reassurance. "Do I look very bad?" she asked slowly and raised her hand in a feeble, mournful gesture to her cheek.

For a moment they sat in silence. He was forced to look without flinching at the dark, withered lips, the webbed, ashen cheeks, the pulp of flesh at her throat. He searched her eyes for a vestige of the vigor he remembered but saw only the querulous lids, the pupils peering in terror from the prison of her body.

"Your hair is whiter," he said, "but you look fine."

She shook her head.

"I'm not well," she said drearily. "I can't eat anymore and can't hardly walk."

"Chester still at the mills?" he asked to divert her attention from herself.

"He's doing what he'll always be doing," his mother said. "Working in the mills and with your sister entering contests to win new cars and washing machines and t.v. sets. When they come home they eat and watch some t.v. and go to bed. They don't have a dozen words to say to each other or to me."

He recalled the lean and weary frame of his sister and the stolid, gentle man she had married. In the years he had lived with them he marveled at the unchanging pattern of their days, work, food, sleep, television, and occasionally, love. From his attic room early in the morning he could hear the creaking of the springs of their bed in the room below, his sister's muted moaning and sometimes a single hoarse cry from Chester. Only in their moment of union did he hear either of them utter a cry to indicate they were alive.

He felt an urgency suddenly to leave, get out into the air, abandon the tight, dismal house as he had fled from it three years before. He rose and his mother reached up to him with a spasm of anguish.

"Not yet!" she pleaded. "Don't leave yet, Alex!"

"Listen, Mama," he said gently. "I've got some important business, one of the reasons I came to town. But I'll be back first thing in the morning."

"I've got some bologna and cheese," she said. "Have a sandwich first and Chester has beer in the icebox."

"I can't now, really, Mama," he said. "I've got to go."

She looked up at him with her naked, glistening eyes. "There are vesper services at church tonight, son," she said. "I don't get to church much anymore. Marika and Chester sleep late Sunday mornings and I can't stand on my feet too long anyway. Can you take me to church tonight?"

He started to refuse, thinking of Miriam, and then his mother's wretched face muted his rejection.

"If the meetings finish early," he said, "and I can get away, I'll take you to church."

"Services start at eight o'clock," she said. "But if we're a little late, it's all right."

"Okay, Mama," he started restlessly for the door. When his hand touched the knob he heard her voice, thin and in the grip of some nameless fear.

"Alex?"

"Yes, Mama?"

"You try, my boy. You try to come and take me to church."

"I'll try, Mama."

He drove back downtown, anxious suddenly and impatient. He parked the car and walked to the small bar a block from Miriam's office where the two of them used to meet. He had a couple of drinks and about four o'clock he phoned her office. He waited in turbulence while someone called her.

"Yes?" Her tone was pleasant and unsuspecting.

"Miriam, it's Alex."

There was a moment of startled silence.

"How are you, Alex?" He sensed her wariness.

"I'm fine," he said. "I'm just passing through town on business and thought I'd call. How are you?"

"Oh, I'm fine," she said.

He heard a voice close to her raised in inquiry and she muffled the phone for a moment and answered. He heard the receiver moved back to her ear.

"Miriam," he spoke her name with a sudden urgency. "I'm at the Zebra down on Michigan. Remember? I wanted to see you, talk to you for a few moments. Can you come over after work?"

"Oh, I'm sorry," she said. "I can't, Alex. Some of us are going out to dinner tonight. I've got to hurry home and dress."

"Listen, Miriam," he said, and felt his throat harsh and dry. "If you could come down for just a few moments . . ."

"No, I . . ." he heard an irritation and hardness enter her voice.

"I've got to leave late tonight," he said. "Just one drink, please."

Someone in the office spoke to her again and she left the phone. He waited in a growing unrest until she returned.

"All right," she said. "I'll be down a few minutes after five. Just one drink."

"One drink," he said, and felt a leaping in his blood because he was going to see her again. He held the phone tightly in his fingers long after she had hung up.

He went back to the shadowed booth and drank a third scotch, feeling his spirit reinforced. He fashioned an eloquent structure of words to tell her why he wanted and needed her.

At five o'clock the door opened, letting in a burst of light, and he tensed. Two secretaries entered, laughing and excited, their miniskirted legs visible for an instant before the door closed. He signaled to the waitress to bring him another drink.

He tried to sort out the memories, the months that he recalled now with nostalgia. Those nights when he'd knock on her apartment door and she opened the door on the chain and peeked out at him, her short taffy-colored hair framing her adorable face.

It's your lover, he would say.

I have no lover, she would say. My husband and five children are asleep. Go away.

I promise not to wake them, he would say. Let me in and I'll give you a present.

What present, she would say.

My hands and my lips, he would say, my body and my heart.

My darling, she would say, and she'd open the door and he'd walk in and they'd embrace, their bodies pressed tightly against one another.

They would eat dinner together, the juicy steaks and the sparkling wine, the two of them seated across from one another at her small table, laughing, touching each other with their eyes, the wine glistening wetly on her lips.

She'd laugh and in a great torrent of words would tell him the events of her day, with the magic to make something special of each ordinary occurrence. She'd use her hands and body and eyes to pantomime the scenes. And he had to laugh with her laughter that came deep from her slender body. Afterwards she'd come and sit on his lap and rest her check against his cheek and whisper her words of love.

"Alex?"

He looked up with a start and Miriam stood beside the booth. He started to rise and nearly upset his glass.

"I'm sorry," he said. "I was daydreaming. Sit down, Miriam. I'll get the waitress."

"I don't really want a drink," she said and she sat down

in the booth across from him. "Let's just talk a few moments."

He stared at her face, seeing the remembered brightness of her eyes even in the shadows, the fine sensual curve of her lips.

"You're still lovely, Miriam," he said.

She stirred restlessly and looked down at the table for an instant. Then she looked back at him.

"How are you, Alex?" she said.

"I'm okay," he said. "I'm just in, like I told you, for a little while. I stopped by and saw my mother and thought I'd give you a ring."

"That's fine," she said.

The front door opened again and several men and girls entered, filling the bar with their shrill and boisterous voices. Miriam looked after them as they slipped into booths across the way.

"Did you get my letters?" he asked.

She looked at him surprised.

"No," she said. "Did you write?"

"No," he said. "I started letters many times and never could put down what I wanted to say. I decided finally I had to come and tell you myself."

She looked down for a moment at her hands, the marvelously gentle hands that made every touch seem a kind of caress.

"It was just as well you didn't write," she said. "There wasn't anything really to say."

"Are you sure?"

There was an instant of strained silence.

"Listen, Alex," she said quietly. "Let's not suffer through one of those nostalgic here-we-are-once-again reunions between old lovers. I'll always be grateful to you. The year we had together was one of the loveliest of my life. But it's over now. The way you wanted it over three years ago."

"I didn't want it over, Miriam," he said. "Not really. But there were all the other things. My mother waiting for me to marry so she could live with us. You don't know what that would have been like. I lived with her and my sister for the ten years after my father died. It got so I couldn't breathe. I had to get away and think things out."

"Whatever the reason," she said. "It's over. Let's just talk for a little while now as old friends."

"Are you happy, Miriam?" he asked.

She laughed her melodic little laugh.

"Dear Alex," she said. "Have you come back to salvage me from misery and spinsterhood?"

"I didn't mean it that way," he said, and felt his face flushed.

"I know you didn't," she said gently. "And I didn't mean to sound cynical. I was miserable and unhappy for a long time after you left. I cried a lot waiting for the phone to ring or for the mail to bring a letter from you. Little by little I began to mend the broken seams of my life."

"Are there different boyfriends or just one?"

"For the last year, just one," she said. "It's not the way it was with you and me, not nearly as crazy and wild. But he's good and gentle and loves me very much. And I love him."

"Do you, Miriam?" he heard the harsh urgency in his voice and was ashamed.

"Yes," she answered quietly. "I love him very much. I know what you're thinking. All the times we told one another that our love would endure forever. But that kind of love exists only in the poems of lovers. Most of us have to make an accommodation with loneliness and with life."

"Does he bring in your tree on Christmas Eve?" he asked. "Do you trim it together with the ornaments we bought? And do you sit in the glow of the lights and drink Lancer's wine from the little long stemmed glasses?"

"It's almost like that," she said calmly. "But not the same." She sat back in the booth, her head erect, watching him.

He was conscious suddenly that the bar had filled, all the stools taken by shadowed forms, a surging clamor of voices and laughter sweeping the room.

"Have you found anybody else?" she asked.

"There have been a few girls," he said. "No one I care about." No one I loved as I loved you, he wanted to say.

"It's good to have someone you really care about," she said. "You know the way I am. I need someone." She raised her arm to look at her watch. "Listen, Alex," she said. "I've really got to go. I'll be late."

"Go ahead," he said.

She started to rise and then stopped and slowly sat down again.

"Don't be angry," she said gently. "If I could stay longer, I would, for a little while anyway. We could have a few drinks together and share all the old memories. But it really doesn't make any sense."

"Nothing much does these days," he said.

"That's true," she said, her voice low and suddenly somber. "When they murdered Bobby Kennedy too, I cried not only for him but for all of us."

"I've felt like that lately," he said. "Nothing makes much sense. I feel that I'm drifting with no port in sight. Because I can't seem to look ahead I think I've begun to look back."

She was silent for a long moment and he had a curious sense of a period being placed carefully at the end of a page he had kept without punctuation.

"I'm sorry," she said. "Alex, I'm sorry. I have to go."

She rose slowly to her feet. He rose to stand beside her.

"That's all right," he said, and shrugged wryly. "Are you going to marry this fellow?"

"We talk about it once in a while," she said. "Neither of us feel anything urgent about it. We live in the same building, different apartments on the same floor. We can be together whenever we went and alone when we want to be."

"Convenient," he said. "I had to drive for miles."

She smiled. "You slept over many nights," she said.

"You cooked fine eggs for breakfast," he said.

She laughed. "You mean burned fine eggs. I was a terrible cook and I'm not much better now."

She put out her small, slim-boned hand.

"Goodby, Alex," she said. "When you're back in the city again, phone me and maybe you and Paul and I can have a drink together." She paused. "I've told him about you. I think you'd like him too."

"I'll phone next time," he said.

She hesitated and then she laughed.

"I was going to kiss you," she said. "But it seems foolish. We've shared so many wonderful kisses, you and I, what use is a little peck in public?"

He smiled against the stiffness in his cheeks. "I'll reach into my memories and pick one more fitting," he said.

She reached out and touched his arm in a fleeting, soft caress. Afterwards she turned and walked to the door, holding her lovely head as high and proud as she always walked. He was reminded of the young hitchhiker of that morning, the same calm, certain step. They both accept life, he thought, and I retreat from it.

The door opened and he saw the glitter of the setting sun mantle her head. He felt an urgent longing to run after her, to cry out that he had returned because he still loved her, still needed her. Instead, he walked unsteadily to the men's room, past the stools and booths filled with laughing, drinking men and girls.

The interior of the church glistened with candles, the air drifting slow and warm scents of incense and melting wax. The priest in his gold and brocaded vestments stood before the altar and raised his long pale fingers toward the cross of Christ.

Alex looked down at the bent figure of his mother standing beside him, a twisted form that might have been carved from the trunk of a gnarled tree. She pressed her hands tightly against the railing before them.

In the pews around them he recognized men and women he knew, looking older, more resigned. He had a strange feeling of the years falling away, standing in the church between his mother and father, memories of coffins closed, candles flickering, elegiac chants, and the sweet taste of communion wine.

The choirmaster's voice rang somberly across the church, the chorus of girl's voices following behind. The priest turned and motioned for the congregation to be seated. His mother leaned against him, her hand gripping his arm for support, and lowered herself slowly to the bench. He sensed her watching him and he turned and caught her with a curious tender joy on her scarred cheeks.

When the collection tray came out he reached into his wallet and brought out a couple of dollar bills. He felt his mother tug at his arm.

"Don't put in too much," she whispered. When the tray reached them he dropped in a dollar and she put in a nickel and a dime.

At the end of the service he took his mother's arm and led her slowly into the stream of people moving toward the portico. She peered anxiously around her for familiar faces.

"Hello, Mrs. Savalas, you're looking fine. How's your family? I'm not so good, you know. I'm sick. Remember my son, Alex? He's come from California to visit me."

She repeated the same message loudly to several different people, pleased when strangers heard and looked toward her and Alex. In the portico as he tried to lead her from the church, she pulled back.

"We've got to see Father Valoris," she said. "He'll want to see you."

They waited in the rear of the church and he shook hands numbly a number of additional times with people who greeted his mother. She stood close beside him, one hand resting upon his arm, a warm pleasure rampant within the slow, stiff movements of her head, absorbing the exultant moments to be recalled countless times later.

When there were fewer than a half-dozen people left in the portico, the priest came from the nave of the church, his long black cassock swirling about his ankles. Alex's mother tugged at his arm, moving them into the priest's path.

"Father, you remember my Alex?" she said with her voice trembling. "He's come all the way from California to see me."

The priest put out his hand and smiled. Alex took it and mechanically, as he had done a thousand times in the past, bent and kissed the back of the palm.

"A long way," the priest said, "but worth it to bring such pride and pleasure to your mother's face."

"All the way from California, Father," his mother said and there were tears in her eyes.

They shook hands once more, and then as the sexton began snuffing out the candles to darken the church, they left.

The four of them sat and drank coffee around the old walnut, diningroom table. His mother, his brother-in-law, Chester, eyelids heavy and mouth twisted in an effort to remain awake, and his sister, Marika, pale lean-fleshed cheeks, and a sullen curl to her lips.

"Well, I think I'll hit the sack," Chester said. "We got a rough rolling schedule tomorrow." He rose and smiled at Alex, extending his hand. "Maybe I'll see you in the morning."

"I'll be leaving tonight," Alex said. "I have to get an early start to make New York by day after tomorrow."

"No, Alex!" his mother said with dismay. "Not so soon!"

"I can't, Mama, I'm sorry," he said.

"At least sleep here tonight," his mother pleaded, her voice whining and distressed. "You can start early in the morning."

He shook his head slowly.

"Let him go, Mama," his sister said. "He says he's got business, so let him go."

"I'd stay but I'm a day late anyway," Alex said.

"Well, if I don't see you, Alex, good luck," Chester said. He smiled at him again and stood for a moment thinking of something else to add. He gave up and said good-night and started wearily up the stairs.

His mother rose heavily from her chair and began fumbling at the plates.

"Leave the dishes, Mama," his sister said sharply. "I'll pick them up."

"I just wanted the rest of the cookies," his mother said and she raised the small platter and held it trembling in her palsied fingers. "I'll wrap them so Alex can take them with him. I know they're his favorite."

"Thanks, Mama," he said. He watched her shuffling weary and slow-gaited toward the kitchen. He looked back to see his sister's eyes fastened in his flesh.

"Can't you even stay with her for one night, you bastard," she said in a low, hoarse voice. "You bastard, do you think the lousy fifty bucks you send each month buys you off everything else?"

He looked at her and recognized the marks of her suffering.

"Has it been that bad?" he asked.

She was silent for a moment, her anger fleeing as quickly as it had come.

"What's bad, what's good," she said with a cold grunt. "She's dying slowly, day by day, falling apart. And I have to watch her dying, listen to her whimper and cry when she thinks no one hears. She can't do more than walk a few steps and can barely dress herself anymore. One of these days she won't be able to get out of bed and I don't know what we're going to do with her then."

"Maybe you can find a woman to come in and look after her," Alex said.

"A woman costs money," his sister said.

"I'll try to send more," Alex said.

"Sure," his sister said. "You send some more."

He rose then and walked into the kitchen where his mother stood packing the cookies in a small box. He reached around her and picked one up and popped it into his mouth. He whistled in pleasure to please her.

"Delicious, Mama!" he said. "I'll finish them before I'm out of Chicago." He paused. "Listen, I think I'll stay tonight. I'll sleep up in the attic if it's okay but I'll have to leave first thing in the morning."

Her face crinkled like paper, each fold trembling with joy.

"Marika!" she called to his sister. "Marika! Alex is staying tonight. Get sheets for his bed upstairs." She looked back at him. "For one night," she said softly. "It'll be like it used to be. I'll hear your steps and close my eyes and sleep better because you're here."

He lay in his bed in the darkness of the attic, listening to the silence of the house. A branch brushed against the roof and he felt the familiar almost forgotten sound deep in his body. On the street below a car passed and the headlights swept the ceiling of his room with a beam of light. A car door slammed and a dog barked.

Somewhere on the road to San Francisco, the young hitchhiker who was 1 A sat awake or slept in the dark, rocking bus. In their bedroom below the attic Chester and Marika lay together in heavy, burdened sleep. In the small corner bedroom, his aging, dying mother lay comforted by his presence for a single night. And across the city, Miriam's warm, naked body consoled the body of her good and gentle Paul.

The trees made a dry, soughing sound. He settled himself deeper in the covers, turning into himself, remorseful about his mother. He might stay for a little while and try to comfort her. Then he knew he could not stay. We only love those who can still save us, he thought. He turned and faced the wall, thinking of Miriam, wishing it were dawn so he could rise and leave.

Dark Eye

Dark Eye

My father was a drunkard. Every two weeks when he received his wages from the owner of the grocery where he worked, he'd begin making the rounds of the taverns on the street. In the normal course of his journey, we would not see him for the weekend and even the following Monday. But by ten o'clock on those Friday nights he did not come home, my mother had a neighbor look after me and then went out to find my father. This wasn't a difficult search because there were only a certain number of taverns he frequented. When she located him he would be furious at her for pursuing him, would mock and deride her before his companion sots. She endured his tirade silently, until, momentarily purged by his outburst and after purchasing several bottles as hostages for the weekend, he allowed her to lead him home.

He drank steadily through Saturday and Sunday. I kept fearfully out of his way but he ignored me, hoarding his revilement for my mother.

"Tell me, woman!" he cried. "Tell me what devil's blindness made me choose a wife like you, a dried fig, a bloodless stone, a deaf and dumb bitch!"

It seemed incredible to me, even as a child, that anyone might wish to abuse my mother. She was a slender and lovely woman with a complexion so pale and fine that tiny violet veins were visible just beneath the surface of her skin. She spoke softly and moved with a lucent grace. Sometimes, playing alone, I felt a longing to look at her and I'd go to find her in another room, sit close beside her for a while, warm and nested in her presence. The moments I treasured most were those we shared when she sat before her mirror at night, brushing her long glistening hair that was dark as a blackbird's wing. I watched her then with a curious tension in my body.

My father was a tall, burly man who might once have been regarded by some as handsome, until indulgence and self-pity had scarred his face with weak, ugly circles. Whether drunk or sober, he moved in a shuffling and uncertain walk, defeat and failure rising like a fetid mist from his pores.

Although he worked at many different jobs, never able to hold even the menial ones for very long, he regarded himself as a Karaghiozis, the profession he had practiced in the old country, a puppetmaster of the shadow puppets once so popular throughout Greece. The art of the Karaghiozis was handed down from father to son and my father had learned his craft from his father. As a young man in Greece, he performed frequently at festivals and fairs, but the popularity of the plays declined. Just a few years after he married my mother, the plays were being requested only on a few special holidays. A new generation of children turned to other pursuits and only the old and infirm lamented the passing of the Karaghiozis.

My father must have come to America thinking that in the new country of myriad opportunities, he would be able to practice his craft. But the children who had never seen a Karaghiozis had other allegiances to Laurel and Hardy, Buster Keaton and baseball. And their parents were too involved with the artifacts of home and the rigors of business to bother with an old-country art.

Once, when I was eight or nine, and this was the only time, I remember my father performing the Karaghiozis. It was in the week before Christmas and I sat in the assembly hall of the church with perhaps a hundred other children on long low benches around me. A scattering of adults sat in chairs along the walls. On a small platform in front of us was a rectangular screen of thin, translucent muslin.

When the lights in the hall were turned off, the room was totally darkened except for the radiant screen casting eerie flickering lights across the faces of the children. From behind the screen came a rattling sound, as if pieces of wood were being shaken in a sack. A few men clapped, and then on the glowing screen a palace appeared, a courtyard and gardens, and in the foreground, a fountain. The brightly attired figure of a soldier appeared. He pranced a few steps and then cried, "Karaghiozis! Wake up, Karaghiozis! The sultan is coming!"

From behind the fountain snapped a great bald head, the face in profile containing a single huge dark eye. The head drew back down for a moment and then the silhouette of Karaghiozis leaped swiftly into view. A powerful body with one arm shrunk to no more than a hand emerging from his chest, the other arm long and apelike.

The sight of the weird figure caused the children to cry out, and with a wrenching of my flesh in fear, I joined my shriek to their cries.

A frantic sequence of scenes followed, characters appearing who shouted, danced, sang, quarreled, laughed and beat one another. There were dancers and beggars, soldiers and wrestlers, fishermen and sultans, gods and devils, a rabid throng inhabiting the screen with a violent and teeming world that my father created and controlled. His nimble hands directed their leaps and jumps and somersaults; his voice delivered their cries, harsh, shrill, tearful, deceiving, demonic. Above all the players loomed the figure of Karaghiozis, his dark eye piercing the screen. It seemed to look directly at me and I screamed in terror even while the children around me shouted and shrieked in glee.

When the lights went on at the end of the performance, I sat mute and exhausted. A vigorous clapping brought my father from behind the screen, his face flushed with power and triumph as he bowed, acknowledging the cheers and the applause. He stood afterward in the center of a group of admiring men, who slapped his shoulders and shook his hands. My mother hung smiling to his arm. I went to her to be consoled for my distress, but even while she held me against her body, I felt her love directed only toward my exultant father.

He never performed the Karaghiozis in public again. In the years that followed, he kept the cardboard figures of the players, perhaps twenty-five or thirty of them, in a footlocker at the rear of his closet. Sometimes, when he was drunk, he would pull out the footlocker, open it and sit down on the floor beside it. He would bring out the mad Karaghiozis and all his companions. He'd spread them around on the floor, pick them up, move their heads and arms. They often spoke only in his head, but when he could not contain himself, he cried voices between them. In the end, exhausted and unfulfilled, he would store them carefully away and go lamenting to his bed.

My father lost his job in the grocery, worked for a while in a laundry and then lost that job as well. During this period, my mother took work as a waitress to pay our rent and food. When he could not find money on which to drink, my father spent his time brooding.

I remember a night when my mother was still at work. My father had been locked alone in his bedroom for hours until he called me in. I found him on the floor beside the open footlocker with the Karaghiozis players spread around him. He wasn't drunk then, but his face was flushed and a frenzy glittered in his eyes. He motioned for me to sit beside him and, frightened, I obeyed.

"In the old country," he said, "a father teaches the Karaghiozis to his son. In this way, it is passed from generation to generation. My father taught me and I will teach you."

I trembled and nodded slowly.

"They don't want the Karaghiozis now," my father said with bitterness, "but someday it will be revived. The crowds will gather again and cheer and laugh and cry out for Karaghiozis." He looked at me with burning eyes. "You must be ready for that time."

He motioned to one of the cardboard players. "This one is Hachivat, Karaghiozis' friend; and this is Celebit, the dandy; and Tusuz Deli Bekir, the bellowing bully; Tiryaki, the opium smoker; Zenne, the dancer . . . and this one, this one is Karaghiozis."

He picked up the cardboard Karaghiozis and held him tenderly in his hands. I had never seen him look at any living creature with the warmth and love his face held as he looked at Karaghiozis. He moved slowly to hand the figure to me. "Hold him now and I'll show you how to control his head and arms."

The huge dark eye in the profiled face terrified me and I shrank away.

"What's the matter?" my father cried. "What are you afraid of? He won't hurt you! This is Karaghiozis!"

His anger fled and he tried to speak softly to reassure me.

"It will take time to teach you all the plays," he said. "You must learn them slowly and learn them well. Then you will be able to improvise plays of your own." He stared at me with naked and earnest eyes. "Do you know that once I could continue a dialog between Karaghiozis and his friend, Hachivat, for more than fifteen hours? Do you know that once the mayor of our village, watching me perform, hearing Karaghiozis talk of politics, the mayor offered me a position in his office? Do you know . . . ?"

His voice trailed off as he looked sadly at my locked and frightened face.

"Get out, little bastard," he said wearily. "Get out of my sight. Go to bed."

I hurried from the room to undress and climb shaking under the covers. I called to my mother when she came home and she came and sat beside me, consoling me by her presence until I had fallen asleep.

That night marked a change in my father. His last hope had fled and he seemed more furiously bent on his own destruction. His credit was dried up at the taverns on our street and he made futile pilgrimages to other neighborhoods. When he could not bully or steal money from my mother or my cousin Frosos, he begged and borrowed from friends and strangers along the street. Abandoning all efforts to find any kind of work, he whirled in a wind of drunken despair.

Any redeeming memory I had of him, any bond of blood remaining between us was demolished in the blustering, whining, raging moments when he cursed fate, the misfortune of his marriage, the madness that made him leave the old country. And in his frenzy his voice altered, becoming shrill and hoarse, taunting and pleading, demanding and denouncing, as if all the myriad tongues of the Karaghiozis players were crying through his lips.

My mother suffered as he suffered, prayed for him constantly and accepted all his curses and imprecations in silence. On those evenings when his helpless rage seemed to be tearing him apart, my mother said my prayers with me and put me to bed. She closed the doors between my room, the hall and their bedroom. I still heard faintly my father shouting and cursing for a while. Then a silence fell over the rooms, an ominous and terrible silence, although I did not understand until years later the way in which my mother took my father's rage and frenzy into her own frail body.

Once, only once, did I condemn my father to my mother. I was about twelve and it was after one of the worst of his rampages, when he had broken several dishes he knew my mother treasured, and finally, like a great beast, had collapsed in a heap on the floor. He lay sprawled on his back, his mouth open, harsh drunken snores erupting from his loose, limp face. I whispered a wish to my mother that he might die.

She had never struck me before, but she beat me then. She beat me savagely with a belt while I screamed in shock and pain.

"Listen to me," she said, her face white and her eyes like knives. "Say such a thing again and I'll have the flesh hot from your back. In the old country your father was an artist, a great Karaghiozis. They came from villages a hundred miles away to see him perform. Now nobody cares for his skill and he rages and drinks to forget his grief and loss. Do you think a man whose soul is being torn apart can help himself? We can only love him and have faith in him. He has nothing else."

But I could not understand, and for turning my mother against me, for the beating she gave me, I hated him more.

My father died when I was fourteen. During one of his drunken sprees in the coldest part of winter, he had stumbled and fallen in an alley. The snow began and the thick flakes covered him. He lay concealed for hours until he was discovered. They took him to the hospital and called my mother. For three days and three nights, while he struggled to die, she fought to hold him to life. On the morning of the fourth day, cousin Frosos took me to the hospital. We walked the long ward filled with beds and strangers, and at the end, behind a screen, my father was dying.

He was curled on his side, one half of his face hidden, one arm extended in a twisting grasp for something that seemed just beyond his reach. His cheek was unshaven, his huge dark eye open, staring straight ahead. My mother, her face worn like a river stone by tears, led me to the bed and put my hand upon my father's hand. I felt the quiver of his flesh expiring under my fingers.

He could not turn his face to look at me, but the eye stirred restlessly. He looked no different than I remembered him many times before. He was helpless, the way I most favored him, because at those times he was unable to curse or to strike my mother.

Cousin Frosos led me away from the bed, and at the screen, I stopped and looked back one last time. A fly buzzed over my father's head and the dark eye in the dying face burned in a frantic effort to escape and follow the wings' swift flight.

I awoke that night to hear my mother scream. She was still at the hospital with my father, but I clearly heard the howl of desolation and loss that came torn from her soul. I knew my father was dead.

Through the following months, my mother grieved. Only forty, she seemed to age a year with each month. Still she worked and took care of me. I took a job after school and on weekends, and when payday came, I gave my mother every dollar that I made. In addition, there was a lodge insurance policy on my father's death that provided us a small regular monthly sum. Strangely, as survivors, we lived better than we had lived when my father was alive. We might almost have been happy then, for the first time in my memory, except for the way my mother grew swiftly older, quietly, irrevocably mourning my father's death.

Sometimes late at night, when she thought I was asleep, I would see the light burning under her bedroom door. I would quietly open the door a narrow crack. She would be sitting on the floor, the open footlocker beside her, the cardboard figures spread across her lap, her hands holding, her fingers fondling the wild, dark-eyed Karaghiozis.

When I finished high school, I received a tuition scholarship to a college several hundred miles away. My mother and I accepted the separation. I wrote her at regular intervals, telling her about my classes, the news of school, and avoided letting her know about my loneliness, the ways in which the past locked me in a shell I could not break. Her letters were brief, filled with admonitions for me to study and pray and live true in the eyes of God. Each time I saw her after the separation of a few months, I marked again the ravages of premature age, her hair grown dove gray, a web of wrinkles gathering around her eyes, a gauntness at her throat.

When I graduated from college and walked to receive my diploma in a black cap and gown, my mother sat in the third row on the aisle, an old woman watching her son in his moment of fulfillment. I went to hug her afterward, holding her slim, frail body in my arms, wanting her to share the achievement she had helped make possible. Yet, in that moment, I held only a fragment of her in my arms, and with a cold chill sweeping my heart, I realized how faint a hold she retained upon the earth.

It was only a few months after my graduation that my mother died. She was less than fifty and should have had many more years to live. But she had no relish for life, and after I finished my schooling, her last bond to the earth was gone. She fell ill in the spring, lingered only a day and died as quietly as she had lived for the past eight years. It was as if the shadow she became after my father's death was suddenly brushed away by a light gust of wind.

I buried her, as she had wished, in the cemetery beside my father, one of two graves beside the stone fence. They would lie together forever, with no one to shield or console her against his abuse.

And on the same day she was buried, I carried the footlocker to the basement of the building in which we lived, and in the furnace, one by one, I burned the cardboard figures of the Karaghiozis' puppets. Hachivat, Celebit, Tusuz Deli Bekir, Tiryaki, Zenne, the beggars, soldiers, sultans, wrestlers and devils, all consigned to the flames. Karaghiozis himself I saved for last, and when the final fragments of the others had gone up in ashes and smoke, I put him into the flames. I knelt before the furnace door and watched trembling as his arms and legs curled and writhed and darkened in the fierce fire, his limbs shriveling in a final anguished spasm, his glowing dark eye suspended for an instant of torment after the rest of the figure was gone.

My father was a drunkard, a bastard who beat and abused my mother. Yet she loved him more than she loved anyone else on earth, remained true to him for the death in life, and in the end, joined him for the life in eternity.

How strong the bonds of faith, how deep the abyss of devotion. And how terrible and unfathomable the love that welds a man and woman together forever.

the Waves of Night

the Waves of Night

That Sunday morning in late March, Father Manos rose, as usual, before daylight, not shivering quite as much as he had on previous Sunday risings for months. He walked to the window and pushed aside the curtain to peer out. Darkness still covered the sleeping city, misted stone and brick peaks of buildings, a single ring of light under a corner lamp. For the first time it seemed to him he could hear the heart of the earth beating faster, a thin promise of early spring, a forerunner of green feast and fruitfulness in the weeks ahead.

He washed and dressed briskly and left the house, walking the deserted streets to his church as the fragmented dawn glimmered across the roofs and parapets of the city.

The shops he passed were shadowed and silent, the taverns that had throbbed with revelry a few hours before, padlocked now, their muted neon signs creaking gently in the stillness. A tomcat emerged from an alley, fur ruffled and wary, idling its way home after a night of errant and promiscuous love. I will expect you at confession, Father

Manos thought wryly, as the unrepentant rake glided by.

Even inside the church, sombrous and damp with the chilled shadows of the night, he seemed to feel the stirring of the earth beneath his feet. Then, with a laugh, he realized that it was the old sexton, Janco, raking up the coals in the basement furnace. Soon the old man would come up and begin lighting the candelabras before the icons of St. John the Baptist, and the Holy Mother with the Child-Christ. In another few hours the great chandelier would be lit and the light representing the stars in the sky would shine down upon the nave full (well, almost full) with the members of the congregation.

It was his custom in these quiet and serene moments to pray. He knelt before the Royal Gate of the Sanctuary, the portal decorated with the icon of Christ as Shepherd. He prayed for the end of the war in Viet Nam, for the starving children in Biafra, for the welfare of the poor, for the general condition of the country. He prayed for the wellbeing of his parishioners, for the perpetuation of the faith, and, finally, he spoke a prayer of gratefulness for the plenitude of his own life.

He was fifty-nine, in good health although somewhat overweight, and with (some exceptions, unfortunately) a good parish. It was true there were a few of the wealthier parishioners with an unholy penchant for distressing him. There was the peculiarly Greek conception of the priest having to spin like a dervish to fit the parishioner's vacillating moods and needs. He had, over the years, managed to balance these unreasonable demands in a way that produced a minimum of resentment. The blessed St. John himself could not have accomplished more.

Not all of the priests in the city were as fortunate. Father Peter of St. George's Church was caught between two rabid factions in his parish, one seeking to banish him and the other to retain him. Father Theodore of St. Dionysios was also in trouble although it was common knowledge that he gambled and drank. But many of the weaknesses which the priests developed were not really their fault. The young priests came from Pomfret and Brookline, eager to serve their flocks and God, but their years of prayer and study provided no inkling of what they would find in their new parishes. The malicious, envious individuals, the myriad groups in reckless rivalry, the constant bickering, the vanity of the wealthy and the resentment of the poor, all took their toll.

Our priests are forced to wear the masks of clowns and fools, the savage Father Grivas of Holy Trinity Church often cried. He responded by affixing a single fierce and unrelenting demeanor to his own face, ignoring the angry threats of his trustees to petition his removal. That he was able to remain in his pulpit and serve as priest was simply due to the fear in which they held him. They regarded him as a ruffian, capable of murder if he were crossed or betrayed.

Wasted effort and lost energy. Father Manos tried to counsel him. He met similar problems with a more subtle and political response. He did what he could and if this were inevitably less than was expected of him, he apologized earnestly for his infirmities.

Playing their dirty, hypocritical game, Father Grivas would storm at him, but Father Manos saw no reason to whirl in a tempest of anger and bitterness when some amicable diplomacy could smooth issues out.

The sexton, Janco, came up from the basement into the church. He was a crooked-limbed old man who moved in a disjointed scramble of elbows and knees, his speech all but limited to mumbles and grunts. He lived in a room in the basement of the church and did not require more than a few dollars a week for food. Father Manos supplemented the meager wages the trustees gave the old man with a little money from his own salary, but he found him an ordeal. Now he directed him in the lighting of the Kandilia and patiently pointed out several pews that had not been swept. By that time the first of the black-garbed, stony-faced old women appeared bringing a Prosforon, the offering bread he would use in making communion. Another old woman brought in a small plate of Kolyva, the boiled wheat garnished with raisins and almonds, a reminder that the dead will rise again as the wheat which is buried in the earth sprouts out and bears fruit.

When it was time for him to dress for the service, Father Manos entered the Deacons' door into the anteroom adjoining the Sanctuary. He slipped on his Stiharion, the long tunic that covered his body from the shoulders to the feet. He put on the stole, belt, cuffs and the felonion, the scarlet vestment cape, kissing each holy article before adding it to his person. By the time he had finished tying the cords and ribbons, the first young acolytes appeared in the anteroom on the opposite side of the Sanctuary, slipping noisily into their white altar gowns. He caught the eye of one of them and waved sternly for silence.

"Good morning, Father Manos," Elias, the choirmaster said, as he entered the anteroom.

"Good morning, Elias," Father Manos said.

The choirmaster, a handsome man with pomaded hair that glistened in blue-black swirls, changed into his cassock.

"Looks like a good turnout this morning," he said. "They should fill the collection trays."

"Let's first fill their souls," Father Manos smiled.

The choirmaster left the anteroom and a few moments later his strong and resonant voice chanted across the church.

Father Manos entered the Sanctuary. "Blessed is our God, always now and ever . . ." he whispered. He adjusted the Evangelion and the candlesticks on the great marble Holy Table. He motioned the young leader of the acolytes to silence all movement and speech and then he took his place before the closed panel of the Royal Gate. He folded his hands gravely.

In another moment the old sexton, his brittle, awkward frame harried as usual, rushed past the acolytes into the Sanctuary, crossing himself clumsily, taking up his place at the Royal Gate. When given the signal he would slide open the panel and Father Manos would stand revealed in the total firmament of the church, all eyes drawn through the charismatic union of crosses, icons and candles to him. It was a moment that he had always, secretly, and he admitted honestly to himself, vainfully, cherished, imagining the resurrective effect of the sanctified light across his colorful and brocaded vestments. Behind him the great Holy Table and large wooden crucifix on which the carved, life-sized body of Jesus Christ was nailed, heightened the effect.

The sexton crouched with his skinny arms against the panel, his scrawny old rooster's neck twisted toward the priest. Father Manos nodded somberly. The old man grimaced in a violent effort to match the high solemnity of the moment and slid the panel open slowly, making certain as Father Manos had often warned him, to keep his own figure hidden. The glitter of the church burst across the priest's head. He raised his hands slowly. The congregation filling the benches in uneven rows rose with a sound of woodwinds for the beginning of the Mass.

At the end of the service he divested himself of his vestments, the young acolyte leader helping him. He put on his black cassock and walked from the anteroom to stand on the Soleas, the elevated section of floor between the Sanctuary and the main part of the church. He felt the pangs of hunger rumbling in his stomach and quickly appraised the number of people waiting to see him. There were about five or six, no more than usual, but he had somehow hoped to be spared even that number today. Then he sternly admonished himself for his impatience. Lantzounis would wait, would indeed expect to wait. The luncheon his good wife prepared for them would be even more delicious when they finally sat down to eat.

He motioned toward the group. Hesitantly, the first man walked forward. He was a poor visitor, he said, from another section of the city, asking for a little money to buy food and clothing. He had the uncertain manner and nervous demeanor of the chronic alcoholic. Although there was a contingency fund that would have allowed Father Manos to give him a few dollars, he brusquely promised instead that one of the church organizations would send the man a basket of food and some articles of used clothing. The man left unappeased, mumbling a disappointed thanks. Father Manos was pleased to see a second man among those waiting leave with him.

The second parishioner to come up was a man in his late fifties, stocky and broad of build, with thick gray hair. Father Manos had seen him in church a number of times but could not recall his name.

"I am George Yalukis, Father," the man said in a harsh, anxious voice.

"I know you, Mr. Yalukis."

The man nodded gratefully.

"You know my son, Sam, Father," Yalukis said. "He played baseball in the GOYA tournament last year."

"I remember Sam," Father Manos said. "A fine boy and a splendid athlete."

"Father," Yalukis leaned forward slightly and lowered his voice. "I don't know what to do. Last week Sam got notice to go into the army. He's been 1 A and passed his physical. But he won't go. Says he'll go to jail first."

"Why won't he go, Mr. Yalukis?"

"I don't understand him, Father," Yalukis said. "He talks about the war in Viet Nam being wrong, things like that."

Father Manos shook his head somberly.

"These are difficult times for a young man, Mr. Yalukis," he said. "No youth wants to go to war but to serve one's country is a solemn obligation and responsibility. If he refused and went to jail it might ruin his life, place a stain upon him for as long as he lives."

"I know, Father," Yalukis grimaced as if he were in pain.

"Try to explain that to him," Father Manos said. "Explain how serious the whole matter is, the catastrophic results. Meanwhile I'll say a prayer for him as well as for you and your family."

The man stood staring mutely at the priest. What does he expect of me, Father Manos thought uneasily. What more can I tell him now?

"Father," Yalukis looked shakenly down at the tips of his shoes and then raised his head. "Can you come over with me to my house now, to talk to him? He came home today to see his mother, not me, but he won't stay long. If you could come and talk to him . . ."

Father Manos wavered. He found it more and more difficult to communicate with many of the young people in his parish, particularly the militant and unreasonable ones. He might go with Yalukis to talk to Sam but would probably accomplish nothing if the youth's mind were already made up. Yalukis, obviously a strong-willed and stubborn man, had probably totally alienated his son. How could the priest be expected to pacify him?

"I'm sorry, I can't come now," he said regretfully to Yalukis. "I have another appointment. But tell Sam I want to see him, ask him to come to church and see me tomorrow."

Yalukis shook his head silently and patiently as if he were resigned to his fate. He bent and gripped one of the priest's hands and kissed the back of the palm. He turned and started walking slowly and dejectedly down the center aisle.

For a moment watching his retreating figure, Father Manos felt pinches of remorse. There were so many problems he was helpless to resolve, one aging man trying to administer to a parish of more than four hundred families. Did they want his blood as well as his flesh and bone?

He sighed and looked up at the small windows in the dome of the church. The sky gleamed a vibrant blue through the panes of glass. It seemed to him a bird winged past with a shimmering grace. The winter had been long and hard, he had felt it like a cold stone in his body, but the spring was coming. There would be sun to warm his bones and the scent of flowers in the gardens and the laughter of children on the walks.

"Father Manos?"

He turned back to the church and a young woman stood at the foot of the steps of the Soleas. He recognized Angela Fotakis, a plain, pale-cheeked girl over thirty. Her father, Kostas, was one of the wealthiest men in the parish, owner of four large resplendent restaurants, a substantial contributor to the Coal and Easter offerings.

"Yes, my dear?" Father Manos said.

"Father, my parents are waiting outside," she said. "I've only got a minute." She stared up at him with watery eyes.

"They have found a man willing to marry me. He's old . . . more than fifty." She paused, stricken suddenly by what he might feel to be rudeness.

Father Manos smiled to console her. "Don't fret," he said. "My graying hair and arthritis have made me immune to the vanity of thinking over fifty is young."

"I'm sorry, Father," she said. "I know I'm just past thirty now. I know what they tell me is true, that no other man may be found who wants me if I wait. But I hoped . . . at least . . . for someone just a little younger."

"I know the man your parents are considering," Father Manos spoke earnestly, and with a measured degree of caution because of her father. "He is a good man who will be a good provider. If he is not as young as you wish, that is, after all, not his fault." He took her hand between his palms, felt her fingers tense and chilled. "There are worse things than marriage to an older man. You could marry a young wastrel, a drunk, someone who would beat you. Would youth compensate for cruelty? I know, my dear. We have several cases like that in our parish now." He felt the disquieting rumble of hunger widening in his stomach. "You think about it a little more. Measure the benefits against the disadvantages. I'm sure your good parents would not make you do anything against your will. Let me know what you decide. If you think the aspect of the man's age too distressing, come back and see me. I'll promise to talk to your father."

Angela nodded slowly, her face still pensive and sad. He reached out and patted her cheek gently. She smiled faintly and turned and started toward the narthex.

Father Manos hurried back into the anteroom and slipped off his cassock and put on his suitcoat and coat. He noticed a button hanging precariously on one sleeve. Iota would have to sew that on.

He emerged from the anteroom again. "Janco!" he called, and his voice echoed across the silent church. When there was no answer he called again more sharply, "Janco!" An instant later the old sexton came stumbling out of the shadows.

"I'll be at Mr. Lantzounis' for lunch," he said. "Remember we have a baptism for four o'clock. See that everything is prepared. I'll be back a little after three."

The old man nodded dolefully. His face seemed incapable of cracking a smile. Iota at home and this grim old devil here, Father Manos thought. They were enough to age a man before his time.

But sitting at the head of the bountiful Lantzounis table, Father Manos felt young and ebullient. The platters were heaped with grape leaves stuffed with rice and meat, broiled chicken in a lemon-butter sauce, tureens of creamy avgolemono, leafy green salads with black olives and chunks of white feta cheese and loaves of warm, crisp-crusted bread. There were, as well, several decanters of chilled retsina wine.

He bent his head and blessed the table and the family, his palate quivering with anticipation. When he raised his head the silence was broken by an eruption of amens and hands moving swiftly through the stations of the cross.

"Eat, Father!" Mrs. Lantzounis cried. "Eat and drink

now and relax." She was a cheerful, incredibly obese woman with a roll of fat around her neck so thick it resembled a collar of fleshy fur.

Father Manos patted his midsection. "I have too much weight here now," he said. "Iota starts me dieting every week."

"You're just right, Father," Lantzounis said. "Let me refill your glass." He was a tall, handsome man with strong arms and dark, curly hair. It was common gossip throughout the parish that Lantzounis had a mistress, a young Spartan girl who worked in the office at his meat packing plant. But looking at his poor wife, Father Manos thought, how could one blame him? The rule against adultery must still be tempered by justice. That was the difference, he had always felt, between an enlightened priest and a clerical fanatic.

Sixteen-year-old Caliope Lantzounis whispered into the ear of her sister, Aspasia, and then broke away to giggle shrilly.

"What's so funny, young lady?" Lantzounis snapped.

"Leave the child be, Cleon," Father Manos smiled. "At her age all of life is a source of mirth. I laughed often when I was sixteen." He looked at Aspasia, slender and lovely and dark-eyed. "And at eighteen."

"Have some more wine, Father," Mrs. Lantzounis said. With his mouth full of grape leaves he could not answer but motioned eagerly to his glass.

The wine warmed him and he saw the great bulk of Mrs. Lantzounis flitting with the grace of a nymph around the table, filling plates over again, and pouring endless glasses of wine. The hunger of his stomach was fully appeased. He could feel the wrinkles filled out with the warm, savory food. He managed to stifle a belch and decided, regretfully, that he had eaten enough.

The girls rose in a few moments to help pick up the dishes. They wore print dresses with frilly skirts, modestly miniskirted. As Aspasia bent beside him to pick up his plate, her skirt rose up her legs and he caught a glimpse of her bare white flesh above the hem of her silk stockings. He felt a sudden frivolous impulse to pat her slender bottom.

The urge was disquieting. It is the wine, he thought. The barriers that age and the habit of abstinence had erected crumbled like faulty dikes under the flow of the juice. It was true that what had once troubled him a great deal, now bothered him rarely. He was immensely grateful for the quietude of his body, something achieved after considerable hardship. Even now it was never completely dead. There were vagrant moments when it returned to trouble him and he found himself prickled by the most carnal thoughts.

There was the magazine he had confiscated from an eighth grader in the parish school some months before. In the privacy of his office he had leafed through the pages and was shocked at the photographs of totally nude women in incredibly suggestive poses. His first reaction was one of outrage against the publishers and then he considered sending for the boy to give him a thrashing. But he remained rooted in his chair, the magazine in his hands, his feelings suddenly changing. A curious lassitude settled over his limbs. He saw the breasts of one woman, not as young as some of the others, a certain maturity in the proportions of her flesh, in her dark prodigal nipples. To sleep at night, he thought, against such breasts. To feel the warmth of them against my back in frozen winter. He stared then at his hands, at the fingers and the palms. They seemed desiccated and bloodless like the hands of the saints in the icons. He imagined them caressing the breasts of the woman in the magazine and he groaned and snapped the magazine shut and tossed it into his bottom drawer. But the vision continued to burn him and he opened the drawer and took out the magazine and using all his strength he tore it into pieces too small to tear any more. He threw them into the wastebasket beside his desk. He looked down at the torn pieces and felt a curious and plaintive sense of loss.

"Father?" Lantzounis' voice startled Father Manos from his reverie. "What were you thinking of?"

Father Manos looked into the laughing face of Aspasia staring at him with a certain intuitive wisdom and he felt a rush of blood to his cheeks.

"The wine," he said loudly, in an effort to cover his disorder. "The wine has made me drowsy."

"A cup of coffee then," Mrs. Lantzounis said and she emerged from the kitchen carrying a silver coffeepot and Caliope followed her carrying a great silver tray laden with powder-sugared kourabiethes and honey-nut baklava.

"Mercy!" Father Manos cried with such vigor that they all laughed with him, their voices blending into a happy and harmonious warmth.

Father Manos returned to church some time later than he had planned and found the parents with the child to be baptized waiting. He donned his robes quickly and assembled the relatives and friends in the baptismal corner.

The baby was a girl of about eleven months, a fair and plump child with a fuzz of golden hair. The godfather was Spiro Marketos, President of the Board of Trustees of the church, a man who had made a fortune by speculating in real estate.

Father Manos found him a pompous and insufferable man always determined to have his own way. On a few occasions they had quarreled but for the most part they observed a certain wary truce. Because Marketos was the godfather, Father Manos would be obliged to attend the celebration dinner following the baptism, although he had no more desire for additional food and drink. He also knew, unhappily, that Marketos was fascinated with the sound of his own voice, punctuating his tedious speeches with countless "now in conclusion's" and never ending.

The moment came during the ceremony to immerse the baby under the water in the baptismal font. It was a time for Father Manos that contained all the mystery and beauty of faith. That this naked, squirming pullet of flesh, only some months removed from her mother's womb should now be receiving the sacrament of baptism and anointed with oil in the sign of the cross, filled him with fervent satisfaction. He tried to remember, holding the baby in his arms, the number of infants he had baptized in the past thirty years. A few of them endured the ordeal silently but most screamed shrilly in outrage, thrashing their small limbs violently. He had learned to hold them firmly and gently, without fear, and dunked them for a second, completely under the water. He enjoyed the pleased murmurs that came from the watchers as the body of the infant emerged from the water, dripping and breathless, to be enfolded in the warm, fleecy towel.

When the baptism was over, Father Manos congratulated the parents and relatives. Marketos looked at him with a certain bovine haughtiness. "You are coming to the reception, of course?" His tone suggested no other action would be tolerated.

"I am coming," Father Manos said and within himself sighed.

He sat at the table of honor staring out upon the half-dozen tables grouped together in the private diningroom of the luxurious Regis Hotel. The pleasure of eating and drinking he had sustained earlier in the day had vanished and he found the presence of so much food suddenly repugnant. He reproached himself for not having eaten less earlier and left a margin of space. He sipped his champagne without savor. Simple good Greek wine would not do for any child that Marketos baptized.

"... now in conclusion," Marketos said, for the fifth time, and it seemed to Father Manos that the buffoon had been talking for hours. "I want to relate to you how I came to baptize this lovely baby. Her dear mother, daughter of one of my closest friends, the distinguished owner of the Salonika Laundry, came to see me. She had already been to church to visit Father Manos ..." Marketos paused and looked toward the priest, half perhaps for confirmation and half to ascertain whether he was paying attention. Father Manos sat up a little straighter and nodded although for the life of him he could not remember when the girl had come to him.

"I could discern at once the young lady was troubled," Marketos paused to allow the audience time to absorb the sensitive attunement of his perceptive powers. "She told me there was a young man she wanted to marry."

God have mercy, Father Manos thought, that was more than three years ago. No wonder I couldn't remember. Will the simple flit never stop?

". . . now in conclusion." But by then the voice of Marketos faded into an intermittent mumble and the stain of wine spilled on the tablecloth nearby made Father Manos remember the wine glass the girl's father had shattered when he learned the boy she wanted to marry wasn't Greek. For a year the father had not spoken to his daugher, remaining angered and embittered. Not a trace of Marketos all that time but Father Manos had argued and pleaded the cause of the young people. Now the father sat beaming on the other side of Marketos, all rancor and animosity forgotten, the son-in-law's managership of a lucrative Ford agency helping to obliterate the parental wrath. All the hours of anguish they caused me, Father Manos thought, and now they sit here like lovers, their souls entwined in each other's arms.

He was conscious of a sudden oppressive silence. He looked up startled to find Marketos glaring at him, the eyes of everyone else in the room on him as well. I listen to him faithfully for forty-five minutes, Father Manos thought unhappily, and the moment my attention lapses, the booby quits.

"Our esteemed Father Manos works too hard in his spiritual duties," Marketos said with an edge of malice in his voice. "He finds it hard to remain awake, or perhaps I speak too long, is that it, Father?"

The crowd laughed goodnaturedly and for a fleeting moment of bravado, Father Manos considered saying, yes, that is true, Marketos, you go on and on like a cracked old record and say nothing. But his courage subsided quickly into the rigid propriety of his position and he rose to his feet.

"Forgive me, Mr. Marketos," he said gravely. "I was carried away by your eloquence and moved by your recollections. When you spoke of the day Demetra came to the church to see me, I was reminded of that fateful hour myself, my own feelings as she informed me of her wish to marry this fine young man . . ."

The parents beamed. Demetra clapped her hands in delight and embraced her husband. The guests joined in applause. Marketos sat down to nurse his defeat. Father Manos could not refrain from a sly feeling of triumph. O I can play your game, he thought gleefully, when you cross lances with me, you nincompoop, you had best bolster yourself with a sturdy rod shoved up your starched backside.

Then, ashamed of his vengeful incontinence, he lowered his head and with sincerity invoked the benediction, wishing the guests, the parents, the grandparents, the baby, and yes, even Marketos, a long and fruitful life.

At eight o'clock that evening there was a meeting of the Daughters of Sparta where he spoke concerning the needs of the Boston orphanage. At nine, a half-dozen members of the picnic committee met in his office at church to discuss plans for the Hellenic Federation picnic in July. By the time they had finished a little after ten o'clock, Father Manos was exhausted and Rexinis, one of the members, drove him home.

He walked wearily up the steps of the house he had left near five that morning. He took off his coat in the hallway and went into his study. He sat down in his armchair and bent burdensomely to untie and remove his shoes. He wiggled his toes, unbuttoned his trousers and leaned back in his chair uttering a deep fervent sigh. He yearned suddenly for bed and for sleep.

There was a brusque knock on the door of his study and without waiting for his answer, Iota entered. She was the withered, almost bloodless old lady who tended house for him, an ancient crone with hard blue veins webbing her parchment flesh.

"A call for you, Father," she said and blinked in annoyance at the open buttons of his trousers. "They phoned the church just after you left."

He sighed again, a vexed, loud sigh, not caring that the old lady heard and pursed her thin lips in disapproval. He rose heavily and walked to the hallway for the phone. He had been pleading for a year for an assistant rector to replace young Deacon Botsis who had been transferred to a parish in Atlanta. The trustees were reluctant to pay another salary and the only concession they made was to allow him a priest to help him during the Christmas and Easter holidays. Meanwhile he felt his life being shortened by the excessive burdens and demands of the parish.

The call was from the floor nurse at the Mercy Hospital with a message from Peter Kramos. His nine-year-old son, suffering from leukemia, a boy that Father Manos had visited several times in the hospital and twice given communion, was dying and not expected to survive the night. His father requested the priest to come.

Father Manos slipped his swollen feet back into his shoes and buttoned his pants while Iota called for a cab. He felt a surge of pity for Kramos and his wife, the anguish of parents losing a young child. At the same time he could not help thinking there was nothing he could really do besides join them in their suffering. He had been witness to death many times over the years, felt it a blessing for the aged and incurably ill, a cessation to their suffering. But there was nothing more shattering than the death of a child and at such times he whirled in a helpless desperation to find words to console the bereaved parents.

Carrying his small bag containing Bible and chalice for communion, he walked down the steps to the cab. They drove through the darkened streets. By the time they reached the hospital and he paid the driver, making sure to get the receipt he would turn in to the parish treasurer at the end of the month, his weariness had been submerged under a determination to meet the ordeal ahead.

He was taken by a nurse to the eighth floor. As he came out of the elevator he recognized the boy's uncle who had come to the end of the corridor to grieve alone. His face was stained with tears and when he saw Father Manos he bent and pressed his lips fervently against the back of the priest's hand. Father Manos embraced him silently and walked down the corridor to the boy's room.

The child lay almost lost within the huge bed, only his thin, frail face visible, a thatch of dark hair against the stark whiteness of the pillow. A white-coated doctor stood at the foot of the bed and on either side were the parents. Mrs. Kramos with her hands pressed to her mouth to stifle her moans. Peter Kramos staring down at his son with a mute and terrible grief.

Father Manos looked at the doctor who slowly shook his head. The priest moved closer to the bed, pausing a moment to console the mother. He placed his bag on a chair and removed the chalice for communion. He read a brief prayer and then raised the chalice and with the tiny golden spoon forced a little sip of the bread and wine between the boy's blue lips. The liquid bubbled for a moment from the child's mouth, running a thin scarlet line down his chin. At that instant the child shuddered, his mouth opened, his small teeth glittered in a frightful grimace. After one short shrill explosion of breath, he died before their eyes.

Father Manos almost cried out in shock at the abruptness of the end, only moments after he had entered the room. If the taxi had been delayed even five minutes, he thought frantically, the child might already have been dead when he arrived. Then he remembered the father and mother and looked at them with stark compassion. The doctor had moved from the foot of the bed and bent over the boy. The mother stared uncomprehending at her son. The father took a step closer to the bed and stared down in disbelief. He pushed the doctor aside and put his big hand against his son's frail throat, his fingers touching the boy's flesh in some taut and ghastly effort to revive him. A low hoarse moan broke from his lips and he put his mouth down over his son's mouth and screamed against the pale still lips.

The mother wailed and Father Manos embraced her, the tears burning in his own eyes. He led her from the room while the doctor tried to draw the father off the body of his son. The uncle hurried past Father Manos and the mother to enter the room.

Father Manos helped the sobbing, shuddering woman up the hall. She tried once to turn and go back but he urged her gently and firmly toward the small waiting room at the end of the corridor. He made her sit down and tried shakenly to console her.

When he looked up, the doctor and uncle were bringing Kramos into the room. His face was still shattered, his eyes anguished, the image of the boy's dead face torn across his cheeks. Father Manos left Mrs. Kramos and went to him.

"God bless you in this moment," he said fervently. "God sustain you, my dear friend . . . provide you the strength to endure your terrible loss . . . may God console you with his balm of compassion . . ."

For an instant Kramos stared at the priest as if he were not really seeing or hearing him. Then his face seemed to break apart. He opened his mouth and with a kind of horror Father Manos saw the scream trying to break free. Then Kramos lashed out his fist and struck the priest in the face.

It was a terrible blow. The priest felt his senses cracked apart and as he fell, he cried out in shock and fear. He landed sprawling on the floor, the room rocking wildly around him. His arms flew up in a weird broken flutter of his fingers. He saw the face of Kramos swooping down to attack him again.

The doctor and uncle grabbed Kramos. In his wild fury to get to the priest he dragged them along. His wife screamed and ran to fling her arms around her husband's throat, dragging the weight of her body against his lunge. For a few moments their arms and bodies held him, the three of them barely enough, while in terror Father Manos scrambled to his knees looking vainly in panic for a way to escape.

"Goddam you priest bastard!" Kramos screamed. "Goddam your God! Goddam animals who let my son die!"

They struggled to hold him while he screamed and raged and another intern and orderly came. They dragged him from the room into a vacant room across the hall and closed the door which could not shut out his screams.

A nurse and doctor came to Father Manos where he still huddled on his knees. They helped him to his feet and he heard the solacing voices dimly and to every question he could only shake his head. They washed his face and offered him a bed to rest in, but he begged for a cab to take him home. They took him down to the lobby and called a cab and a nurse offered to accompany him but he insisted on riding home alone. He did not remember getting out of the cab or paying the driver. He fumbled in his pocket for the key and could not find it. He rang the bell. The sound echoed back shrilly and he looked fearfully behind him at the shadowed street. When there was no answer from inside the house he knocked loudly and urgently against the wood.

Iota finally opened the door, drawing a robe about her gaunt body, mumbling complaints about being awakened. He hurried past her up the hall to his bedroom. He entered and closed and locked the door. He sat on the side of his bed and for a long time did not move. Iota knocked on the door and spoke to him. He did not answer. After a while, still grumbling, she left him alone.

When the rooms about him were silent, he rose and undressed. In his underwear he slipped into bed. He pulled the blankets to his throat and shivered. He slid his hands down across his stomach and gripped his genitals. He held himself tightly in a trembling frenzy. Great waves of cold followed by surgings of heat swept his flesh.

"O God," he whispered. "O God, why . . . O my God, why?"

He could not have slept more than a few moments when something startled him, a strange bursting within him and he cried out in terror. He felt sleep abandon him as if it were a soul leaving the body of someone dead. He flung off his covers and rose and left the room. He had a sudden fear of being left alone and he made deliberate noise in the kitchen hoping Iota would wake and come to scold him. At that moment he would have been grateful for even her skinny shanks in their cotton stockings and the sour line of her bloodless lips.

He returned to his bedroom for his robe and then back in the kitchen heated some milk. He sat at the table sipping it, the silence whirling in circles that grew tighter around him. He looked at his hands and was suddenly conscious of them in a way he had never been before. The myriad lines of the palm that laced together in a weird and disturbing pattern, a dark vein pulsing beneath the pale skin of his wrist.

He walked to the bathroom, relieved himself, and felt a burning in his organ. He let water run into the basin and soaked his face with a cloth. He saw his reflection in the glass, the raw ugly bruise that discolored his cheek.

He stared at his face silently for a long time and then felt another sweep of terror rack his flesh. It started in the small of his back, a knife between the ridge of his buttocks, and traveled up as if a frozen blade were rending his body. His mouth opened, his tongue and teeth appeared, and then he screamed . . . not very loud, but thinly and shrilly striking the tile walls and falling back upon him. He put his hands to his ears and felt them as if they were wounds.

I am going mad, he thought. This is the way it must begin.

When the first light of dawn broke over the city he looked up from his Bible with an exhausted relief. He leaned back in his chair and for the first time in hours dared close his eyes. When he opened them the light had spread, glinting across the bedposts and the bureau. He rose wearily and left the room.

In the kitchen, Iota turned from the stove to confront him sullenly.

"What's the matter with you?" she asked sharply. "You rushed in last night like the devil was chasing you and I heard you moving around all night. I couldn't sleep a wink."

"I'm sorry," he said. He stared at her waiting for her to identify the bruise. But she looked at him without a sign that she noticed anything unusual. "You want eggs or oatmeal?" she asked shortly.

"Nothing," Father Manos said, and turned away uneasily, his fingers rising to touch his tender, swollen cheek.

He started toward the bathroom, his muscles sore and cramped from sitting up through the chilled night. He felt the ache with a grim relief, a physical pain that had its origin in something he could understand.

When he moved before the vanity mirror, he hesitated with apprehension. The bruise was clearly there, a raw, red-black blemish that marked his face like a leper's taint.

The remainder of the reflection that stared back at him was familiar, the soft and ordinary face he had known for many years, changing only as age changed it. Yet he saw it now with every vestige of dignity and grace stripped away. The thinning gray hair that he wore long and brushed to cover the area of scalp that was balding. The arched, wry line of his eyebrows above the sockets of his indecisive eyes. The small brush of ridiculous mustache under his nose. Every wrinkle and fold, dreary and common.

For a while he considered remaining at home. But as the morning wore on and he could not sit or rest, he dressed and left the house for the church. He kept his head lowered and his collar up in an effort to conceal the bruise.

In the church he went at once to his office and closed the door. The parish secretary was visiting her mother in Denver, but Janco had heard him entering and brought him several messages from people who had called. As he handed them across the desk to him, Father Manos waited again anxiously for the old man to see the bruise. But the sexton merely stood waiting for some command, shifting from one crooked leg to the other. The phone rang again and with a peremptory motion of his head, the priest signaled the sexton to take another message. Then he fled into the church.

It was dark and sorrowful in the nave, only a few forlorn candles flickering before the icons. He walked through the Deacon's door to the anteroom and from there into the Sanctuary. He stood motionless for a moment in the dry, ascetic air, absorbing the Evangelion, the Blessing Cross, the candlesticks, the Ark for the Sacrament of Communion.

He went to the small basin and washed his hands. Before the Oblation table he began to prepare the communion. He cut out the middle square of the Prosforon and pierced the bread with the lance. He poured water and wine into the chalice and cut the square of bread into tiny pieces, for the Holy Virgin, for the Saints, for the Bishop, for people living or dead, for himself. He put the pieces of bread into the chalice and spread the coverlet over it. He kissed it and prayed to God to accept and sanctify it.

He removed the coverlet and with trembling hands raised the chalice to his mouth. The wine tasted warm and sour on his tongue, trickles seeping into the pockets of his cheeks.

Through the configuration of his arm and the chalice he saw the wooden cross on which the Saviour, Jesus Christ, was crucified. He stared up at the pierced palms and at the anguished countenance and felt a burning in his soul.

"O my merciful God," he whispered to the figure on the cross, "tell me thy name." He held the chalice numbly in his fingers, his voice faint and shaken in his ears, "I pray you, tell me thy name."

He waited in an entombed silence, feeling the pounding of his heart. From the rear of the church came the sexton's hoarse voice summoning him. He was reluctant to leave the Sanctuary, moving further back into the dense shadows for concealment. The sexton came to the anteroom door and called him again and he walked out to answer the call.

The hours of that day passed unlike any he had ever experienced before. He spoke to the visitors who came to his office, feeling his features altering stiffly from frown to wan smile, hearing the words he spoke echoing as if from far away. He was conscious of talking with his head lowered, one cheek turned aside, his fingers raised often to conceal the bruise. Yet no one seemed to notice it, or if they did, made no sign. And the mystification of that veiling fed his disorder.

When the last visitor left, he rose and in the doorway of his office saw the narthex empty. Through the single lone paned window in the corner he marked the fading light and his terror of the night came storming back.

Back in his office he noticed on his calendar that he was to meet Father Grivas for dinner at the Hellenic Cafe that evening. Earlier in the week he had planned to cancel the dinner with the savage priest but he was grateful now that he had not. He phoned the Holy Trinity Church, afraid Father Grivas might have forgotten about the dinner, and asked him if they could meet a little earlier, as well. The other priest's harsh voice agreeing filled him with a measure of consolation.

Father Manos instructed Janco to lock up and then hurried through the twilight streets. Entering the Hellenic Cafe, a shabby grocery and restaurant, he passed the counters filled with dark green and black olives, ripe white cheeses, and crisp crusted breads. He usually paused to enjoy the plethora of food, often buying some to take home with him. Now he walked directly into the shadowed back room. There were a dozen booths lit only by candles that masked the drab and faded cloths. He sat down wearily in one of them, grateful for the shadows and the dimness. When a lean-hipped waiter with a soiled apron tied around his waist came for his order, he asked for a bottle of retsina. As the waiter left the booth, Father Manos saw the other priest.

Father Grivas came striding through the shadows, pulling off his coat on the way. He was a big, stocky man in a shapeless, dark suit. His hair hung shaggy and unkempt over his clerical collar. He had a swarthy, pocked face and a full-lipped mouth that he twisted into a sardonic grimace of greeting.

"It's been a long time," Grivas spoke in a rumbling voice, "since I've heard anybody so eager to see me."

The waiter reappeared with the bottle of retsina, Grivas stared up at him in irritation. "Don't just stand there, boobhead," he said. "Bring another glass." As the waiter walked away, he added. "That one would make a great Deacon." He stared sharply at Father Manos.

"You don't look well," he said. "Did you have a meeting with your damn Board of Trustees?"

"I didn't sleep well last night," Father Manos said. He kept his face averted slightly in an effort to conceal the bruise even though he was not sure the other priest could see it. At the same time he felt a swift, compelling yearning to reveal his terror. He restrained himself with an effort. Like a child, he thought for a vexed moment, like a child I will blurt out all my absurd fears. "It's nothing," he said impatiently. "Insomnia that bothers me now and then."

The waiter returned with another glass. Grivas filled both glasses with the wine. He handed one to Father Manos. "Drink up," he said, "and then drink some more. You'll sleep soundly tonight." He dismissed the waiter with a sharp cutting motion of his hand. "Get lost until we want you," he said.

They sat together drinking for a long time. Some men they knew entered the restaurant, ate dinner, and then left. Instead of eating dinner themselves, they ordered another bottle of retsina. Father Manos was aware he was drinking too much, that other patrons were staring at them, but after a while he didn't care. The wine warmed him, relaxed his body, seeped into the dark, hidden hollows of his distress.

Across from him, Grivas drank steadily, pausing only to order still another bottle when the second one was empty. Although a wilder glint entered his eyes, he showed no other visible trace of the amount of wine he had consumed.

"They are plump and well-fed, shallow and mundane," Grivas said.

"Who?"

"Who else?" Grivas curled his heavy lip with contempt. "You know damn well who I mean. Our blessed brothers in white collars, wallowing in their sties."

"They haven't done you any harm," Father Manos said.

"Just seeing and hearing them harms me enough," Grivas said stridently. He refilled his glass. The wine spilled over the rim and sloshed across his fingers. He raised his big, hairy hand to his mouth and with his tongue recoiling swiftly between his teeth, licked his fingers. "But the fault isn't theirs alone," he said. "They reflect the nescient cretins who make up their congregations. Forced to pander to every idiot who throws a stinking dime into the tray, they become freaks themselves, lambs who live with snakes so long they learn to shed their skins."

He made a move to refill both their glasses. Father Manos tried to stop him with a half-hearted gesture that Grivas brushed aside.

"You are a relentless man," Father Manos said slowly.

"Relentless and cruel. A shade of compassion would make all these frailties bearable."

"I have compassion for them," Grivas growled. "The compassion Herod had, and that is more than they deserve."

With a sudden resignation Father Manos remembered he had heard all these denunciations many times before. He raised the glass of wine to his mouth and took a long swallow. The liquid flowed down into his body, into caverns where his organs lay inert and still.

"I tell the bastards where to go!" Grivas struck the table with his heavy fist and the glasses jumped. "Gluttonous swine wallowing in food while millions starve! Pimping merchants obsessed with spoils while children burn in Viet Nam! Coming to me on Sundays to absolve them of their filthy, necrophilic sins! I'll send them to hell! Let them ask for absolution there!"

"Grivas," Father Manos said, and suddenly he did not care how he might sound to the other priest, "Grivas, something is happening to me."

Grivas fell silent, his chest still heaving in agitation. His harsh breathing grew calmer and he stared at Father Manos with a wary curiosity.

"I don't know what it is," Father Manos said. "I have the feeling it began with a nightmare but I can't be sure." He looked for a long moment helplessly at Grivas, then slowly turned his bruised cheek into the candlelight.

Grivas looked at him silently.

"You see nothing?" Father Manos said. He put his hand to his cheek and felt the tender swollen scale of the wound.

"What should I see?" Grivas asked.

"Nothing," Father Manos said, and shook his head, and felt a flare of panic rising in his gullet. "I'm afraid I'm losing my mind."

For a long moment Grivas did not answer. When he finally spoke, his voice was a shade less harsh.

"Why shouldn't you lose your mind?" Grivas asked. "You wouldn't be the first priest who did, especially in these times. I know one cleric who has twice slashed his wrists and another who tried to conduct his Sunday services stark naked."

Father Manos closed his eyes and held them tightly shut. He fumbled for his glass of wine and raised it to his chilled lips.

"I'm weary and alone," he said. He opened his eyes and stared across the table at Grivas. "The God who was with me as a child, who grew with me as a man, as a priest, he's suddenly hidden from me now."

"Some modern priests think God is dead," Grivas said with a shrug. "That's the new faith now."

Father Manos shook his head slowly. "I don't think he's dead," he said in a low, shaken whisper. "I think he's examined my spirit and my heart and found them wanting. He has turned his face from me because I'm not worthy. He is no longer my rock."

Grivas looked down with an uneasy shrug. "I don't know what's happening to you," he said. "It could be many things. Despair, loneliness, fear and trembling. A man can go on mouthing the clichés for just so long and then a part of him caves in."

"I'll go and see a doctor," Father Manos said, and he clutched at that thought as if it were a raft in the whirlpool of his soul.

"Go ahead," Grivas said. "He'll probably find something wrong to reassure you, but your trouble won't be over then." He finished the last of the wine in his glass, the end of the third bottle and wiped his mouth roughly with the back of his hand. "I think you're a moderately decent man who has suddenly awakened to the absurdity of the whole charade. The pious frauds and bleating hypocrites that you try to anesthetize with candles, incense and dull sermons."

Father Manos felt a sudden ripple of anger in his body, welcomed it for the assault upon his despair.

"Are you any less of a hypocrite?" he asked, feeling the words bitten through his teeth. "Are you any less a fraud than the worst of priests? Tell me that, Grivas!"

"I'm as bad as any of them," Grivas said quietly. "With one difference. I admit my worthlessness and accept my hell. I don't fool myself with false hopes and futile dreams of sacrifice or service. Like the poor priests trying to find meaning in their lives who march with the blacks in Mississippi and get their heads broken by rednecks, or the priests who march into draft boards and pour blood on the files in protest for Viet Nam and for that Christian exercise are sentenced to rot for ten years in some filthy prison with cutthroats and thieves. Leave your pulpit and raise your voice and they'll burn you or crucify you." He paused, a wry grin twisting his lips. "But that might be your salvation," he said. "Join the marchers and protesters. There's always room for a benign, grayhaired martyr."

Father Manos looked shakenly at Grivas. "Once I marched in such a group," he said slowly. "With Negroes into a white neighborhood. They screamed and cursed us and the Rabbi walking beside me was struck with a brick. I panicked and ran. I was sick for three days, told everyone it was the flu, but it was simply terror." He shook his head wearily. "I'm afraid," he said. "I've grown old, soft and afraid."

"Screw them all!" Grivas said, his face dark with a rush of blood. "Let them devour each other! In the end we may leave the earth as clean as it was before Adam and God's curse!"

Father Manos stared at him in shock and wonder.

"How do you live, Grivas?" he asked. "How do you endure your days and nights despising yourself and all other men?"

Grivas looked at him without answering. He rose soddenly to stand swaying for a moment beside the booth and then clutching his coat, turned and walked unsteadily toward the exit. At the door he paused. After a moment he started back to the booth, reached it and bent forward, putting his hands on the table for support. His face was close enough for Father Manos to smell the rank pungence of wine, close enough to see the marks of suffering like dark etchings around the priest's eyes.

"I live on my hate," he said, and the anger and bitterness were gone from his voice, a terrible anguish in their place. "Hate alone keeps me alive."

After Grivas had gone, Father Manos remained at the table for a little while. His knees trembled and he was afraid that if he tried to walk, he would fall. Finally, he rose and left the restaurant, surprised how quiet and desolate the streets were. He was anxious to reach home and the pavement tossed under his legs as if it were the deck of a ship on a stormy sea. He looked vainly for a cab, peering with apprehension at the occasional car that rumbled past as if it contained parishioners who would recognize him. A drunken priest, he thought helplessly, a drunken priest who will fall into a gutter where they will find me in the morning.

But he did not fall down. After a while the night air, cool and damp with the faint scents of spring, cleared his head. He raised the collar of his coat about his ears and walked with his head lowered, charting the path his steps would follow. At each corner he raised his head to take a renewed measure of direction.

Then he stood before the house. He walked up the steps with a silent, grateful prayer that nothing had happened to him on the way. He found his key and fumbled it into the lock and opened the door. In the dim hallway he was assailed at once by the staleness of the rooms around him. The thin mist of cologne the old lady sprayed under her fossiled arms and upon her withered breasts. His own odors, dry, thin scents of prayer and flat, rheumatic spoor of aging, useless flesh.

He went to his bedroom and pulled off his topcoat and suitcoat together. He unbuttoned and removed his collar and took off his shoes. He pulled up the blanket from the bed and lay down and covered himself with it. He lay curved on his side, his head bent forward, his knees drawn up almost into his stomach. Dear God, he thought, merciful God, let me sleep.

Whether because of the wine or his exhaustion from the night before, he slept. He woke with his head buried in his pillow and could not be sure the length of time which had elapsed. For a moment he was stung by the fear it might still be night. He kept his eyes tightly closed and raised his head slightly to listen for some familiar sound. When he heard nothing he tensely opened his eyes a slit and with a spasm of gratitude opened them completely. The rim of window around his shade was bright with sunlight. He rose quickly from the bed, remorseful at his terror of the night before, ashamed when he remembered drinking with Grivas.

The shower spray struck his naked flesh with a piercing satisfaction. The water ran in torrents down his legs and into the drain, flushing the crust of despair from his body. As he was dressing, Iota knocked brusquely on the door of his room. He asked her cheerfully to prepare eggs and toast for his breakfast.

His mood of ebullience carried him into the afternoon. A steady stream of parishioners came to see him on various problems and the hours passed quickly. Late in the afternoon a young man and girl came to see him about plans for their marriage. Happiness radiated from their pores and for a while he basked in their joy. After they had signed the necessary papers he walked with them through the narthex to the outer door of the church and outside on the stone steps. They waved to him from their car and he raised his hand in a final flutter of farewell and saw his fingers outlined like the claw of a skeleton against the darkening sky, the first streaming shadows of twilight. He could not believe that the day was already gone and he felt his flesh tighten in a sudden, haunted distress. He turned and fled back into the church.

He spent the evening at home with the television playing loudly, for the first time not minding the inane noise and chatter. Finally, Iota asked him to lower it. She was peeved at him anyway because he had not eaten any of the dinner she had prepared. He tried to engage her in conversation to postpone her going to bed. But she told him she was tired and went to her room.

He went to his own bedroom and brought his Bible back to the parlor. He sat down again and began to read. The words blurred before his eyes. He made an effort to concentrate, speaking the verses out loud. They echoed with a stark hollow ring back in his ears.

He closed the Bible and leaned forward in his chair. He listened for sound in the silence of the house. His tongue felt dry, his throat tight, and he rubbed his palms in quick nervous flutters across the cloth of his trousers. The table, chairs, curtains, all seemed washed in a strange, eerie light. Even a bowl of unripe plums on the table caught the cold sparkle, their yellow glow glaring into his eyes.

He closed his eyes, felt them seal his flesh like the lid closing on a coffin. A great scream burst somewhere deep in his body. He slipped from the chair to his knees and then, unable to help himself, pitched forward to the floor.

Prostrate and exhausted, his body swept by waves of trembling, he began feverishly to pray.

On Saturday morning he sat in an anteroom of the Archdiocese waiting for his appointment with the Bishop. He huddled in his chair, his head down, faintly hearing the voices of people around him. He felt a tugging at his sleeve and looked up, startled, into the thin, pale face of the Deacon.

"You can go in now, Father," the Deacon said. "His Eminence is waiting."

Father Manos rose and followed the Deacon toward the large double doors. The Deacon opened them and he passed into a huge chamber and the doors closed behind him.

Bishop Okas rose from behind his dark-oak desk and crossed the room, his robe sweeping about his ankles. "How are you, my dear Father?" he said. He extended his hand, almost in apology, as if knowing yet regretting that ritual required he do so. When Father Manos bent and kissed the back of his palm, he withdrew his hand quickly as if the gesture of obeisance somehow embarrassed him.

The Bishop was a young man, still in his early forties, with a face and body made lean and spare by prayers and fasts. He had a mustache and a small trim black beard. His face might have been that of any ordinary parish priest but for the way, Father Manos had noticed before, it radiated a capacity for love and devotion, suggesting a grace that came through fulfilling God's will.

"Thank you, Eminence, for consenting to see me this

quickly," Father Manos said. "I know how busy your schedule is."

"Not at all, Father," the Bishop said. "I am always delighted to see one of my brothers in Christ." He motioned to a chair. "Please come and sit down."

Father Manos sat down on a stiff-backed armchair and the Bishop sat down across from him, spreading and smoothing his black cassock across his long, lean legs. His eyes, large, dark and intense, stared somberly at the priest.

"What is it, Father?" he asked softly.

Father Manos raised his hand to hesitantly touch the bruise on his cheek. He had ceased expecting that it was visible to anyone but him, yet now, in the Bishop's consecrated presence he had a quiver of hope that the wound might be seen and healed.

"Something has come to me in the night," he said, and even the words filled him with foreboding, and he made an effort to keep his voice from becoming shrill. "I'm filled with a terrible fear." He shook his head in bewilderment. "I have never known anything like it before."

Bishop Okas listened earnestly. It seemed to Father Manos that a flutter of compassion swept the younger man's face and he was ashamed of his confession. As if sensing his discomfort, the Bishop leaned forward and reached out to touch the priest on the arm in a gesture of consolation. How beautiful his fingers are, Father Manos thought, long and slender and so pale they were almost white. They might have been the fingers of one of El Greco's saints, stretched toward an unfathomable, unreachable height, toward a vision visible only to their spirit.

"I have been a priest so long," Father Manos said. "Spoken so many benedictions, performed so many sacraments. And now I shrink and tremble and fear. Is it because I have failed God? Nothing is clear to me anymore. The night brings phantoms and demons. I feel my soul cry out."

The Bishop stared at him silently. He looked once toward the ceiling and for an instant his finely curved lips were visible within his silky beard. Then he rose, unfolding his body to his lean, full height. He stood with his back to Father Manos.

"Life is a jungle," he said softly. "All around us is murder, avarice, brutality. The jungle is tangled and thick and the animals scream in the dark." He turned slowly to look down at the priest. "But a road runs through that jungle, a rough and stony road that seems to fall away in places, or is sometimes hidden, yet it is still there. The road of faith."

His eyes blazed with a lucent fervor. "You are older than I am, Father, you have been on this road longer, have more reason to grow weary, more reason to feel anguish. These are times more wicked than the time of Sodom and Gomorrah. A bitterness rises through our lives, a nausea, a mist of melancholy, things that sound a knell." His voice fell to a sibilant whisper. "He who loves his neighbor burns his heart, and the heart, like green wood, in burning groans and distils itself in tears. We must understand, Father, that the evil of our suffering can be cured only by greater suffering."

Father Manos looked down at his hands, the soft, trembling fingers, the backs scarred with spots like the back of a toad.

"We can no longer save Man from himself," the Bishop said. "We can only keep the faith alive until He returns, for He must return. Meanwhile we must have a passion for God. It must possess us and fill us with such fire that we are conscious of nothing else. God can keep us in sight of the road. God! Only God! And if we remain on the road, the church will survive, and our Saviour will return to redeem us!" His voice rose slightly and he clasped his hands together and extended them to Father Manos in mute and quivering entreaty. "Let us pray together, Father," he said, and he slipped to his knees before the priest.

The sight of the Bishop kneeling before him swept Father Manos with a fit of trembling. He reached out and clasped the Bishop's fingers and then slipped to his knees on the floor beside him.

"O my God," Bishop Okas whispered. "O my God, help your servant who is in sore need of your light and consolation. Help him, my God, do not forsake him now in his hour of need."

He lowered his head toward the floor. His cassock spread like a mantle about their ankles. His slender shoulders trembled. "Abandon despair," he said. "Abandon anguish. Give yourself freely to God's spirit."

"I will," Father Manos said.

"God is love!" Bishop Okas said.

"God is love," Father Manos said.

"God is light!"

"God is light."

"God is eternity!" Bishop Okas cried.

"God is eternity."

Tiny beads of sweat had formed on the Bishop's forehead, a vein pulsed in his temple, dark with a rushing through of blood. A small bubble of saliva ran from his mouth into his beard. He swayed slightly and let out a great long sigh that seemed to surge from deep in his body.

Father Manos reached to him and bent and kissed the lovely and slender hands again, feeling the flesh moist and warm, a scent of some fragile, delicate greenhouse flower rising from the palms, a flower able to thrive only in compounds of heat and filtered light.

Bishop Okas turned his head slightly and for a moment their eyes met.

He must see me now, Father Manos thought. He must recognize the wound I bear now, in this moment, this unmatched moment when our souls have been joined in a solemn and tender benediction.

But Bishop Okas made no sign that he had seen anything but his own visions. He turned aside and rose to his feet, smoothing down his cassock. Father Manos rose slowly and made his cross and left.

That night, again, he did not sleep. But the frenzy and terror of the preceding nights altered now for him into a strange resignation. In his darkened room he floated upon the waves of night, watching the moonlight curl around the shade of his window, hearing the floorboards creak. In the passage of that night he recalled the years he had lived, unrenowned and unmemorable years marked by futile words, wooden gestures, faltering faith. What had happened to his dreams of life with purpose and fulfillment? He felt his soul poured out like water, his bones out of joint, his heart like wax. He heard a bough blown against the house and raised up his head and quietly prayed for death.

Before daylight he dressed and walked through the darkness toward the church. He heard his short, stiff steps echo on the pavements as if he walked in a great hollow chamber. At the rim of the sky darkness and light raveled their threads.

He unlocked the heavy church door, swung it open, and entered the darkened narthex. He walked into the silent nave and sat down in one of the pews. He sat for a long time staring into the shadows until the shades of dawn lit the ceiling of the dome and seeped down into the hidden corners, unveiling angels and saints, winged and fluted seraphims. The Royal Gate of the Sanctuary emerged glittering from the darkness. From there, blinded in his vanity and pride, he had taken the name of the Lord vainly. If he did not murder, his silence condoned the murderers. If he did not starve the poor, he comforted those who ate while the poor hungered. If he did not burn the innocent, his complacence sanctified the burners.

After a while he rose and walked to the anteroom. He began dressing himself in his robes and vestments for the beginning of the service. He heard the first of the young acolytes entering the anteroom on the opposite side of the Sanctuary. Then the choirmaster entered.

"Good morning, Father Manos," he spoke cheerfully without looking at the priest.

"Good morning, Elias," Father Manos said.

"A lovely, early spring morning," Elias slipped into his cassock. "Winter will be over soon now."

"Yes, Elias," Father Manos said. He walked into the Sanctuary, crossed himself, and took up his place before the closed panel of the Royal Gate. He heard the choir-master begin his chant, the rustling and murmuring of people moving into the pews, the whispering of the acolytes in the anteroom. And in those moments that he listened and waited he understood he would hold his bond to the earth and to his church until it was God's will to sever him from them. He would live joylessly watching the coming and going of the seasons. Yearning for death and peace he would be burdened with mortality, each year like ten he had passed before, the long thin drawing out of his soul to cover them.

But in those years remaining to him he would seek to build again the shattered temple of his faith, seek to renew that vision of something surpassingly fair which had haunted him in childhood, make the words of his mouth and the manifestation of his spirit acceptable in the sight of God.

And if he still failed because he had lived too long with hypocrisy and deceit, then he would bear the bruise on his face and soul for as long as he lived. When he died, he would have nothing to render the Lord but the thin, futile ashes of his suffering.

The old sexton entered the acolyte's anteroom and came

in his broken-gaited jog into the Sanctuary. He crossed himself hastily and took up his crouched position before the panel, twisting his face fearfully and anxiously toward the priest.

For the first time in all the years the two of them had waited together before the panel, FatherManos recognized the sexton's terror. He suddenly understood how each Sunday morning the simple act of pushing aside the panel was a pillory and an anguish for the old man, an endlessly repeated ordeal wherein he might commit some terrible indiscretion before his priest and his God.

"Don't be afraid, Janco," Father Manos said softly, and he reached out to clasp the old man's bony shoulder in a gesture of consolation.

The old sexton gaped up at him numbly for a moment and then slowly, awesomely understood that the priest had recognized and forgiven him his fear, had touched him in absolution. He bent renewed to his task, his crooked, twisted shoulders shaking.

Watching the old man begin to cry, Father Manos felt tears breaking slowly from his own eyes.

He bent his head and as the panel slid open, he saw the tears glitter into specks of flame on the scarlet cloth of his gilded vestments.